Shining Darkness

Recent titles in the Doctor Who *series:*

WISHING WELL
Trevor Baxendale

THE PIRATE LOOP
Simon Guerrier

PEACEMAKER
James Swallow

MARTHA IN THE MIRROR
Justin Richards

SNOWGLOBE 7
Mike Tucker

THE MANY HANDS
Dale Smith

GHOSTS OF INDIA
Mark Morris

THE DOCTOR TRAP
Simon Messingham

DOCTOR · WHO

Shining Darkness

MARK MICHALOWSKI

BBC
BOOKS

2 4 6 8 10 9 7 5 3 1

Published in 2008 by BBC Books, an imprint of Ebury Publishing.
Ebury Publishing is a division of the Random House Group Ltd.

Doctor Who is a BBC Wales production for BBC One
Executive Producers: Russell T Davies and Julie Gardner
Series Producer: Phil Collinson

The Random House Group Ltd Reg. No. 954009.
Addresses for companies within the Random House Group can be found at
www.randomhouse.co.uk.

A CIP catalogue record for this book is available from the British Library.

ISBN 978 1 846 07557 5

The Random House Group Limited supports the Forest Stewardship
Council (FSC), the leading international forest certification organisation.
All our titles that are printed on Greenpeace approved FSC certified
paper carry the FSC logo. Our paper procurement policy can be found
at www.rbooks.co.uk/environment

Series Consultant: Justin Richards
Project Editor: Steve Tribe
Cover design by Lee Binding © BBC 2008

Typeset in Albertina and Deviant Strain
Printed and bound in Germany by GGP Media GmbH

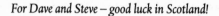

For Dave and Steve – good luck in Scotland!

'Two and a half billion light years,' said Donna Noble, her eyebrows raised and a gentle smile tugging at the corner of her mouth, 'and you've brought me to an *art gallery*?'

'Two and a half *million* light years,' corrected the Doctor, pulling Donna back out of the path of something that resembled an upright anteater, studded with drawing pins, trundling down the street, 'and it's not *just* an art gallery.' He sounded almost hurt.

'If you're going to tell me it's "not *just* an art gallery" because it's got a shop that sells fridge magnets…'

'It might,' replied the Doctor, glancing away guiltily and tugging at his earlobe.

'You,' laughed Donna, 'are *so* transparent, you know that?'

'And you,' cut in a deep, buzzy voice that sounded like a talking chainsaw, 'are *so* in my way.'

Donna turned: right next to them, smack bang in the middle of the broad pavement on which they stood, was a robot. Although it took Donna a few seconds to work that out. From the waist up, it was like a bronze version of some Greek god, all bare metal muscles, jawline and attitude. From the waist down, however, it was a different story: instead of legs it had caterpillar tracks.

Donna's first reaction to it was that it was an ordinary person (well, as ordinary as you could get, looking like someone had vandalised something from the British Museum with a can of metallic paint) who'd lost his legs in an accident and had half a JCB grafted on.

'Sorry,' she said automatically.

'I should think so,' buzzed the robot – and only then did Donna realise that it wasn't a creature of flesh-and-blood. The eyes were cold and glittering, and she realised the skin wasn't skin at all, but a curiously fluid metal, reflecting back, madly distorted, her own face. 'If you're going to stop to converse, I suggest you move over *there*.' And it raised an imperious finger and pointed to the other side of the pavement.

This was too much for Donna.

'Well,' she said, drawing herself up.

('I wouldn't,' she vaguely heard the Doctor whisper.)

'If you're going to be *quite* so rude,' she continued, ignoring him, 'I'd suggest that *you* move over *there*.' She pointed to the centre of the street, where four lanes of traffic were whizzing by at stomach-clenching speed. 'Mate.' She added for good measure.

('I really wouldn't,' added the Doctor.)

The robot raised a haughty eyebrow and looked Donna up and down.

'Organics!' it spat, sneerily.

'That meant to be some sort of insult?' retorted Donna. 'Cos where I come from, sunshine, that wouldn't get you on *Trisha*, never mind *Jeremy Kyle*.'

('Donna…')

'Your words are gibberish,' said the robot dismissively.

At this point, the Doctor cut in, grabbing Donna by the arm and pulling her to one side.

'Donna! When in Rome…'

'Sure you don't mean Pompeii?' she replied, acidly. 'Who does he think he is?'

'He probably thinks he's a local who's just come across two offworlders who don't know the rules and regulations for using the streets, is what he probably thinks.'

Donna saw the Doctor flash a bright, apologetic smile at the robot.

'Don't smile at him – a simple "excuse me" would have done. No need for all that attitude.'

'Perhaps in the future,' said the robot wearily to the Doctor, revving up its gears as its base rotated (although its top half stayed facing them), 'you could train your pet better?'

Donna's mouth fell open but, before she could say anything, the Doctor put a firm arm around her shoulder and moved her out of the path of the robot – which, without another word, roared off down the street.

'Pet?' she gasped.

'Pets are very highly thought of round here,' said the Doctor quickly – but without much conviction.

'*Pet?*' Donna shouted after the creature, but it had

vanished into the crowd. She turned back to the Doctor, open-mouthed. 'Can you believe that? You said you were taking me somewhere civilised and sophisticated. I'd get more sophistication and civilisation at West Ham on a Saturday.'

The Doctor gently moved Donna back against the building, out of the path of the crowds streaming around them.

'For once, I'd like to meet a *nice* robot,' she said, still fuming. 'There must be some. Somewhere. I mean, with the whole universe to choose from you'd think there'd be *one*…'

'Remind me to take you to Napir Prime,' the Doctor said. 'The perfect hosts – well, that's what it says in *The Rough Guide to the Isop Galaxy*. Never been myself, but I've heard good things.'

Donna raised a sceptical eyebrow.

'From the robots I've seen so far, the strike rate's pretty low.'

'Don't judge a whole class of beings from just three examples,' the Doctor chided, checking out the monumental skyscrapers that lined the street. 'Remember how you were when you saw your first Ood…'

'That was different. They weren't robots – they just looked a bit…' She smiled at him, hoping to defuse the tension a little. 'Ood.'

'That's probably what they thought when they saw you.'

He gestured at a glossy, dark green building just a few yards along.

'Come on – let's see if there's any robot art in here. Might give you a new perspective.'

'Not me that needs a new perspective,' Donna grumped as she followed him through doors that said a cheery 'Good afternoon' as they opened.

'Art,' the Doctor began, sounding ever-so-slightly-pompous, 'is a window on the human soul. Or the Andromedan soul, obviously,' he added with a tip of the head.

Donna raised an eyebrow.

A creature a little like a squishy bedside table, with a crown of glinting, metallic eyes, paused in front of them, apparently to observe the slab of dull, grey marble in a glass case that the Doctor was also peering at. Although, Donna realised, it might have been observing *them*. She gave a tiny, awkward smile. Just in case. Having already offended, however unwittingly, an Andromedan, she thought she ought to err on the side of the caution with any new ones she came across.

'If you'd prefer,' the Doctor whispered, 'I'd be more than happy to take you somewhere filled with danger, excitement and death. Your call.'

The bedside table ambled off, making a chuckling, coughing sound.

Donna held out her hands, palms up, weighing up the options.

'Danger, excitement and death?' Her hands moved up and down. 'Art gallery?'

'Philistine,' grinned the Doctor. 'We could combine

the two and visit the Third Stained Glass Empire of – ooh, hang on!'

And suddenly, Donna was standing on her own, watching him dart across the black mirrored floor of the art gallery towards a large display case. With a sigh, she trudged after him. She loved art. Really, she did. She'd had a copy of that sunflowers picture on the wall at home. That was art. Proper art. Not just bits of stuff stuck on a board and sprayed with grass cuttings. Or half a Mini coming out of the floor. Or a slab of grey marble.

She caught up with him, almost colliding with a trio of tall, painfully skinny blonde women who'd just entered this particular room in the gallery. They looked awkward and stilted, their faces impassive.

'Sorry,' she whispered, skirting around them. They watched her go silently.

The Doctor was leaning forwards, his nose squidged up against the display case inside which, on a slender glass spike, sat something that looked like a rusty truck wheel, encrusted with fragments of diamanté.

'Donna!' whispered the Doctor, beckoning her forwards. 'What d'you make of this?'

She peered at it.

'You're going to tell me that it encapsulates the eternal struggle between *The Pussycat Dolls* and *Girls Aloud*, aren't you?'

'That's next door,' he said. 'No – this is much better.'

'Go on then, Sister Wendy, what is it?'

'Well, I don't actually know what it *is*, but whatever it is, it's a bit more than just art.'

'Is it?' Donna tried to stifle the yawn that she could feel bubbling up. The three supermodels – or whatever they were – had separated and were all standing around the exhibit that was so fascinating the Doctor, although he didn't seem to have noticed them. There was something slightly odd about the trio, though: something measured and shifty. Like burglars casing a house, figuring out the right time to nip in and steal the DVD. Never mind the fact that, as far as she could tell, they were all identical.

The Doctor pulled out his sonic screwdriver, activated it, and waved it around near the case. Seconds later, he pulled a puzzled face and popped it back in his pocket.

'Just wait here,' he said, looking around. 'I'm going to find the gallery's owner.'

'Couldn't you just read the brochure?' asked Donna.

'I have. It's rubbish. Back in a sec.'

One of the supermodels, dressed in a plain grey trouser-suit with creases so sharp you could cut yourself on them, glanced at her. She smiled back.

'Art,' she said vaguely, uncomfortably. 'Great, isn't it? Window on the human soul. Or Andromedan soul,' she added for good measure.

The supermodel just stared at her – and then at her two companions.

Art-lovers, thought Donna. *Don't you just love them—*

The thought was cut off as she spotted the greasy patch on the glass that the Doctor's nose had left. In the pristine, snooty environment of the gallery it looked horribly out of place, and Donna was tempted to leave it there.

But she was an ambassador for Earth, wasn't she? She

didn't want the locals going around saying what mucky pups humans (and Time Lords) were, especially with these three women paying such attention to the exhibit. So, whipping out her hanky, she stepped forward to give the glass a bit of a clean – at the very same moment that a wave of prickling static swept across her skin, and the whole room flared brilliant, snowy white.

ONE

'Oi!' shouted Donna as the glare subsided, leaving sparkly traces on her vision. 'What was—'

She stopped as she realised that somehow they'd managed to redecorate the art gallery in the few seconds that she'd been blinded. Instead of a wide, airy space with a shiny black floor and white walls, they'd turned it into a lower, pokier space, all purply-black swirls. The walls around her curved, giving the impression of being inside half a hard-boiled egg. The display case and the supermodels were still there, although the lights inside the display case had gone out, leaving the diamanté truck wheel looking even more like a piece of old junk than it had before. It began to dawn on her that maybe – just maybe – she wasn't in the gallery any more…

Donna spun on her heel as a door hissed open somewhere behind her.

'Oh marvellous!' deadpanned the little fat man with curly blond hair who came striding in. He glared at the three supermodels. 'Absolutely marvellous! Who's *she*?' He plonked his hands on his ample hips and looked her up and down.

'*She*,' snapped back Donna, 'is the cat's mother. Who are *you*?'

'Hold her,' said the man, sneering up at her. Suddenly, Donna felt steel bands tighten around her upper arms and looked to see that two of the supermodels had grabbed her. No one, she thought, least of all supermodels, should be able to hold *that* hard.

'Gerroff!' she grunted, squirming. But their grip was unbreakable. The third supermodel stood on the other side of the display case, observing her with cold, dead eyes.

'Who is she?' asked the man, almost as if she weren't there.

'I'm a woman who happens to know a man who's going to be very unhappy when he gets back and finds out what you've done.'

'She entered the transmat area as we activated,' intoned one of the supermodels in a dull, emotionless voice, ignoring Donna.

'I am here, you know,' snapped Donna. 'I can speak for myself.' She paused. 'Transmat? I've just been *transmatted*?'

'Clearly,' said the little man in a weary voice. He stared at her with pale blue eyes that were almost as cold and dead as those of the supermodels. He wore a lapelless, dark grey business suit with a crisp shirt, striped with pink and white horizontal bands. Something about him made Donna think of estate agents.

'Who are you, anyway?' Donna demanded. 'When the

Doctor finds out, you're going to be in big trouble.'

'The Doctor? Who's she? Or he?'

'Oh, ha, ha. Very funny.' Donna twisted her neck around to try to find the Doctor, but she realised that she'd been transmatted alone.

Her head snapped back round to face the little man.

'What have you done?' she growled. 'Where am I? Who are you?'

The man paused, his eyes narrowed.

'My name is Garaman Havati, and you're aboard the *Dark Light*, my ship. Who are you?'

'Donna Noble. Spelled T R O U B L E if you don't put me back *exactly* where I was. Now.'

Garaman chewed thoughtfully at the corner of his mouth.

'No,' he said eventually. 'I don't think so.'

His eyes flicked to the supermodels flanking her.

'Put her somewhere safe.' He looked back at her. 'I'm tempted to have you killed now, but something makes me think I should keep a hold of you for a while.'

'Oh, mister,' said Donna, struggling as the supermodels began to lead her away. 'You have made one helluva mistake. Just you wait 'til the Doc- ow! Get your hands off me!'

But the supermodels took no notice, and half led, half dragged her from the room.

The Doctor had barely gone five paces when the flare of light behind him made him spin on his heel. Where, moments ago, there had been the display case, Donna and the three humaniform robots, there was now just an empty space and a shallow, rectangular hole in the floor.

'Not again,' he sighed, and then caught sight of the art gallery's attendant, rushing in from the next room to find out what the flash of light had been.

'Excuse me,' said the Doctor to the attendant, a slim man with permanently arched (and, the Doctor suspected, dyed) eyebrows and a look of utter disdain on his face. 'But what just happened there? You don't use Huon particles for anything, do you? I hope she's not going to start making a habit of this.'

'I was hoping,' drawled the man, arching his eyebrows even further as he cast a glance around the room, 'that you would be able to tell *me*.'

'Well, judging by the flash and the missing bit of floor, I'd say you've just been heisted.'

'"Heisted?"'

The Doctor nodded, squatting down on the floor where the display case had been standing and taking out his sonic screwdriver. He activated it and waved it around in the air for a few seconds.

'Heisted,' he said simply. 'By transmat. At least it's *not* Huon particles, then.' He sprang to his feet. 'Someone's just spirited away a valuable treasure.'

'Hardly valuable,' said the attendant dismissively.

The Doctor fixed him with a glare.

'I was talking about Donna. But now you come to mention it, what exactly was that thing? The one in the case.'

The attendant shrugged elegantly.

'Art,' he said simply, as if that were all the explanation that was needed.

'Oh, I think it was more than just *art*, wasn't it?'

'This is an art gallery,' the man said. 'We display art.'

'What you were displaying there,' said the Doctor, 'was a very sophisticated piece of technology, judging by the readings I picked up from it.'

He stopped, suddenly, as he realised that whilst he was standing here, wasting his time debating the gallery's displays, Donna was still missing.

'If you ask me,' he said as he headed for the door, 'you need to boost your transmat scrambling field. This would *never* happen at the Tate Modern, you know.'

And with that, he was gone.

'Scuse me! Thank you! Oops! Ta!'

The Doctor raced out into the street, nipping smartly between the passers-by, until he stood at the edge of the pavement, watching the never-ending stream of traffic and machinery as it flowed past like a river.

The transmat trace he'd picked up with the sonic screwdriver would be fading quickly. And, if he was right about where she'd been transmatted to, it could be just minutes before she was out of his reach for ever.

'Taxi!' he called, leaning out into the traffic and sticking out his arm.

Nothing happened – the cars and trucks and robots just rolled on past. He tried again, but had no more success. Finally, in despair, he shoved his fingers in his mouth and let out an ear-shattering whistle. On the pavement all around him, aliens, humans and robots stopped what they were doing and turned, astonished that such a little thing as him could have made such a noise.

The Doctor was in the midst of pulling an apologetic face when, with a crashing tinkle of bells, something that resembled an armoured, custard-coloured elephant shuddered to a halt in front of him. A golden eye on a stalk extended from the side of the creature's head and came to a halt a few inches from the Doctor's own.

'Do I take it,' said a low, sonorous voice, 'that you are requesting transport?'

'I did say "taxi",' the Doctor said apologetically.

'Ah,' said the yellow elephant. 'You're an offworlder, aren't you?'

The Doctor looked himself up and down. 'Is it that obvious?'

The eye blinked, its 'eyelid' a mustard-coloured iris.

'You announced *yourself* as a taxi,' the elephant said. 'Think yourself lucky that no one took you up on it. You don't look exactly built to carry passengers.'

'You'd be surprised. Look, sorry to rush you, but I have to find a friend.'

'Ahhh,' said the elephant after a moment's thought. 'You'll be wanting the companion district then.'

'No no no, not *that* kind of friend. A particular friend…' He stopped, thinking about Donna. 'A *very* particular friend, actually. I need to get to my ship as quickly as possible.'

'The spaceport?'

'No, a lovely little square with a tall building like a hat-pin.'

'The Court of Tragic Misunderstandings. I know it well.'

And suddenly another custardy tentacle emerged from the elephant's flank, wrapped itself around the Doctor's waist, and lifted him effortlessly onto the creature's back, where a comfy, form-fitting seat was already being extruded.

'Two minutes,' the elephant said, moving back into the traffic seamlessly.

'Couldn't make it one, could you?' asked the Doctor.

'Not without tampering with my speed limiter, breaking half a dozen city regulations and probably causing an accident in which dozens would die, no.'

The Doctor sighed as a seatbelt wrapped itself around him. 'Two minutes it is, then.'

As the Doctor rode away into the traffic on the yellow elephant, he was being watched.

The observer, a raccoon in red hot-pants and a fez, narrowed its eyes, watching the stranger's conversation with the elephant. Its hearing was acute, and it had caught the entire exchange: the offworlder was heading for the Court of Tragic Misunderstandings.

Quickly, the raccoon pulled out a little transmitter, pressed a couple of buttons, and began to speak.

True to its word, the elephant – whose name was Cherumpanch, the Doctor discovered, during the most terrifying race through traffic that he'd ever had – deposited him outside the Court of Tragic Misunderstandings in just a smidgeon under two minutes. Still slightly dizzy, the Doctor began to root around in his pockets for some sort of payment before Cherumpanch realised what he was doing and told him that public transport in the city was free. With its tentacular eye, it examined the rather unappetising item that the Doctor brandished in front of him.

'It's a peanut,' said the Doctor brightly – if unhelpfully.

'Thanks,' said Cherumpanch cautiously, taking the peanut with another yellow tentacle and sucking it inside.

'Earth delicacy,' explained the Doctor, haring away across the grass to where he could see the reassuring shape of the TARDIS, hugged up in the shadow of a wall. 'The only one in this galaxy!' he called over his shoulder.

'Yuck!' said Cherumpanch, spitting the remains of the peanut out.

'You're welc- oh, hello!'

The yellow taxi-elephant was all but forgotten as the Doctor came to a halt a few yards from the TARDIS. Standing in front of it was a three-and-a-half-metre-tall robot – looking like the result of a high-speed collision between a truck and a steel-mill, with disturbingly red-glowing eyes – and a sulky-looking tanned teenager. It was clear that they had no intention of letting him inside the TARDIS.

The TARDIS that was his only way of finding Donna.

'All out of peanuts,' the Doctor said, holding his palms out to them. 'Sorry.'

'We don't want peanuts,' said the boy.

Despite looking like your average 16-year-old, the boy

had eyes harder and wearier than any teenager the Doctor had met before. He had a thin, chiselled face, a tiny diamond set into the side of his nose, and a rather oversized blue and black striped coat on, despite the sunshine.

'Well that's a relief then. I might have half a ham sandwich somewhere, but I've no idea how long it's—'

'You were at the gallery,' the boy interrupted.

'Good eyesight!'

The boy ignored him.

'You saw the exhibit being stolen.'

'Well, not exactly *saw*. More turned around and it was nicked from behind my back. Along with my friend Donna, and if I don't get back inside my ship in a minute or so,' he said, gesturing towards the TARDIS, 'her transmat trace will have faded. So, if you don't mind…'

He tried to slip between the boy and the robot – which, so far, hadn't moved or spoken or in any other way indicated that it wasn't just a huge hunk of steel street furniture – as the boy tapped an ugly black brooch in the shape of a star on his lapel.

The Doctor felt the hairs on his arms stand up as everything glowed white around him.

'Oh,' he said with despair. 'Not ag—'

And then the Doctor, the boy, the robot – and the TARDIS – were gone.

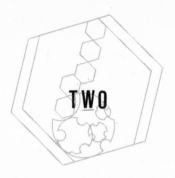

TWO

Donna was starting to get worried. Seriously worried. Fair enough, travelling with the Doctor had its share of troubles. Getting separated from him on this scale wasn't usually one: normally, she had a fair idea of where she was, where he was. And she could usually rely on him finding her pretty quickly.

But this felt different.

She had no idea where she was. Heck, she had no idea where the *planet* was. The Andromeda galaxy, the Doctor had said. Twumpty billion light years from Earth, or something.

Most of the other places that she'd been since she'd teamed up, again, with the Doctor had felt vaguely familiar: Pompeii had been a bit like a theme park, the Ood-Sphere had just been a wintry planet. Granted, the Ood had been a bit strange at first, but the humans there had given the place a sense of familiarity and, in the end, the Ood had been more human than most of the humans. This planet,

Uhlala (if that really *was* its name: she wasn't convinced that the Doctor had understood what the young woman he'd asked was saying), felt unearthly in a way that nowhere else had done: the smells, the sounds, the sights – all of them shrieked 'Alien!' The people walking the streets were bizarre, many of them not looking the least bit like *real* people. And the robots…

Donna's only real experiences with robots had been the robot Santas and the ones on Planet 1. And they were hardly poster children for cuddly, friendly machines. If the ones around here had *looked* like robots – big, googly eyes like headlamps, hissing steam and the like, or cutesy little things like she'd seen on TV – then maybe she'd have felt more comfortable around them. But too many of them looked like living things or weird bits of modern art – or like bronze Greek gods grafted onto construction machinery. There wasn't enough shiny chrome and rust for her to think of them as machines, and, quite frankly, they creeped her out. Especially the supermodels, who, now she'd had time to think about it, were probably robots too. No one that thin and that beautiful had any right to be that strong. And silent. No one that thin in *Heat* was ever that silent. Bimbots – that's what they were: bimbo robots.

They'd dumped her in what was evidently an unused bedroom on the *Dark Light*: all minimal lines, spartan décor (grey and silver – very chic!) and a toilet that had taken her twenty minutes to figure out how it flushed. And they'd locked the door and left her. No amount of banging on it and threatening the little fat guy with what she'd do to him when she got her hands on him had made the slightest difference. She moped around the room, annoyed by the lack of a window (cheapskates, putting her in an inside room), pressed all the buttons on the intercom thing by the bed (no one answered, if it was even working), had a quick wash in the shiny black bathroom, and then flumped down on the bed, all out of ideas.

What would the Doctor do?

Assuming he didn't have his sonic screwdriver (which, of course, Donna didn't), he'd probably rummage around in his pockets, cobble something together out of fluff, string and an old beer mat, and be out of the room in seconds. Donna didn't have any string or beer mats in her pockets (although there was a depressing amount of fluff) and the room was empty of anything that could have stood in for them. She began a careful, inch-by-inch search of the place, just in case someone had dropped a keycard, or there was a whopping great ventilation duct or exposed wires or something. Not that she'd have known what to do with them, but it would have been *something*. She wondered, briefly, if the Doctor's previous travelling companions had ever sat him down and got him to teach them 'Breaking Out of Locked Rooms For Beginners'. She suspected not. It wasn't like they had hours and hours of down-time in the TARDIS. Recently, it seemed like they'd been catapulted from one adventure to another with barely a moment to breathe and get her hair washed. She looked down and plucked at the fur trim of her coat, realising how manky it was starting to look, and wondering whether, by the time the Doctor took her back to Earth, she'd be hopelessly out-of-fashion and everyone would laugh at her in the street. She wondered, idly, if they did dry cleaning in space.

Oh, for god's sake! she thought, launching herself up off the bed. Locked in a room on an alien spaceship on the other side of the universe, and all she could do was worry about her clothes!

'Get a grip!' she told herself, crossing to the door and banging on it so hard that she hurt her hand.

To her surprise – surprise that must have shown on her face, judging by Garaman's (was it Garaman? Garroway? Garibaldi?) expression – the door opened almost instantly, revealing the little man, looking all smug and unctuous. Behind him stood one of the bimbots. For the first time, she could see its cold, unblinking expression clearly and she shivered.

'I think,' said Garaman, entering the room without so much as a by-your-leave, 'we need to talk.' He twirled on the spot and looked up at her. 'Don't you?'

'—ain!' finished the Doctor as his atoms fuzzled themselves back into existence. He turned sharply to the boy and the robot, reassured that the TARDIS had come along with him. 'What is it with you people and transmats? What's wrong with a good, old-fashioned shuttle? I could tell you some stories about transmats, you know.' He stopped and fished the sonic screwdriver from his pocket. 'Now...' He paused and shifted his weight from one foot to the other, narrowing his eyes, before pulling a yoyo from his pocket and experimentally bouncing it a couple of times. 'Spaceship.' He looked at the boy who was eyeing him curiously. 'In orbit? Thought so. Right – where are your sensor controls?'

'Sensor controls?'

The Doctor brandished the sonic screwdriver in his face. 'I need to plug this in before the trace goes cold.' He raised an eyebrow. 'And if you're half as interested in what was stolen from the art gallery as I think you are, if you lead me to Donna, then *I'll* lead you to *that*. Deal?'

The boy considered the Doctor's words for a few moments before pursing his lips and nodding.

The ship, the Doctor noted as the boy led him through the corridors (with the silent robot right behind him) had seen better days. The walls were a dull, steel colour, although half-hearted patches of green and orange paint occasionally shone through the grime and the rust. There was a smell of oil and heat in the air, and every now and again the floor would shudder as though the ship were turning over in its sleep. Or having a nightmare.

'So,' said the Doctor conversationally, over his shoulder, as they trotted down the passage, 'been together long?'

There was no answer from the hulking great machine. For something so big, thought the Doctor, it was surprisingly quiet in its movements. Its face – a broad v-shape of dull metal with no mouth and two eyes that burned like hot coals – looked down at him impassively.

'Mother doesn't speak,' said the boy.

The Doctor pulled a face.

'Not like most mothers I've met, then. Not *your* mother, I take it? What *is* your name, by the way?'

'Boonie,' answered the boy as the door through which they were passing jammed half open and had to be shouldered aside. 'And no, not my mother. It's what she's called.'

They were in the control room: the Doctor appraised it with a quick glance. Shabby, grubby, noisy – but somehow welcoming. A lived-in control room. Not like some of the swanky show-control rooms he'd seen.

'Nice!' he approved as he headed for what were undoubtedly the sensor and scanning controls. A middle-aged woman with cropped, black hair, wearing a stiff, grey uniform stepped forwards, a look of alarm and confusion on her face.

'It's OK,' Boonie said, and the woman dropped back, still not sure.

'I'm the Doctor,' said the Doctor brightly, sticking the sonic in his mouth to shake her hand whilst he used the other to fiddle with the sensors.

'Kellique,' the woman said, throwing another glance at Boonie. 'What's this about?'

'The Doctor is helping us search for…' Boonie broke off, briefly. 'For the exhibit.'

'That what?'

'The *exhibit*,' said Boonie pointedly. 'From the gallery.'

'Oh,' said Kellique, sounding relieved – and a little pleased with herself. 'That. We've got it covered.'

The Doctor's face fell.

'You have? Well, you know how to make a man feel redundant. Where is it, then?' He peered at the display set into the sensor controls and jabbed a finger at it. 'Is that

30

it? Ahhh… so that would put it…' He straightened up, whirled round a couple of times before pointing towards one of the walls. 'About eleven thousand kilometres that way.'

'Give or take,' said Kellique, still trying to work him out.

'And what are we doing about it?' asked the Doctor.

'We're going to follow it,' said Boonie, striding towards a big, raggedy chair in the centre of the room and dropping himself into it. Stuffing was leaking out of the arms, and the Doctor noticed how much of the rest of it was held together with wire and sticky tape.

'Really? Why don't we just use your magic transmat and beam it back out? Along with Donna,' he added.

Kellique crossed to Boonie.

'Who's Donna? Who *is* this man?'

Boonie looked up, his eyes grim and hard.

'They were in the gallery when it was beamed out, according to our agent. They took his friend – Donna.'

'Excuse me,' interrupted the Doctor, joining Kellique at Boonie's side. Out of the corner of his eye, he saw Mother shift slightly. 'But who exactly are "they"? And why did they steal that thing?'

Boonie's glance connected with Kellique's for a moment.

'I mean,' continued the Doctor, beginning a leisurely stroll around the room, 'it's obvious that if a rather sophisticated piece of equipment, posing as a bit of modern art, gets lifted by a spaceship in orbit, then someone would know about it. Are you art police? Is that it? Whizzing around the galaxy foiling art thieves?' He looked around the room. 'A bit *Scooby Doo*, isn't it? And I don't mean to be rude, but you don't exactly look like art police? Not,' he added awkwardly, 'that I'd know what art police look like. But whatever they look like, it's not you lot, is it?'

He stopped. All eyes were on him.

'OK, so now I'm just babbling. But it has given me the chance to examine your control room and to work out that, if you *are* the art police, then art crimes aren't at the top of the local police force's list of priorities. This ship is ancient and falling apart,' he continued, despite the frowns and looks from Boonie and Kellique, 'and is clearly more of a private venture. And, financially, not a very successful one.'

He slapped his palm against his forehead.

'Of course! You're art *thieves*, aren't you? You were casing the gallery when someone slipped in before you and lifted it. That's how you knew what had happened, and how you were waiting for me at the TARDIS.'

'Would it shut you up,' Boonie said, 'if I told you that no, we're not art thieves?'

'It might,' replied the Doctor cautiously. 'Of course, it might just throw up more questions. And if there's one thing I like, it's questions. Prefer answers, mind you, but questions'll do for starters. Like… shouldn't you be *following that ship*?'

The sudden urgency in the Doctor's voice made the two of them turn sharply to the screen set into the arm of Boonie's chair to which the Doctor had pointed.

The moment their attention was off him, the Doctor

was sprinting towards the door and past Mother – but the door had barely begun to scrape open when Mother's huge mechanical hand had grabbed his collar and lifted him off his feet. He swung there for a few moments as Mother turned him round to face Boonie.

'Nice try, Doctor,' the boy almost grinned.

'Well,' sighed the Doctor. 'You know what they say: you don't try, you don't win.'

'And where were you planning to go?' asked Kellique.

The Doctor waved feebly and awkwardly, still dangling from Mother's hand.

'Oh, you know… back to my ship. Out into space. To find Donna.'

'I don't think so,' said Boonie, getting out of his seat. 'Not yet, at any rate. Mother, have his ship – the blue box thing – locked in the hold where he can't get at it. And if he tries anything, hit him. Until he stops.'

Mother lowered him gently to the floor and the Doctor straightened out his crumpled suit.

'Good!' he said, mustering as much dignity as he could. 'Glad we've got that one sorted out.'

'You kidnap me, lock me up in a room without a window – without even a TV! – and now you expect me to have a cosy little chat, do you?' Donna stood with her hands on her hips, glaring at Garaman. 'You heard of psychological abuse?'

Garaman had turned his back on Donna and was strolling around the room, trying to act all cool and casual.

'The Doctor,' he cut in. 'This friend of yours. Tell me about him.'

'I'll tell you about him,' said Donna, 'when you tell me exactly when you're going to put me back where you found me.'

Garaman looked over his shoulder at her and made a sucking noise with his teeth.

'That might be a bit of a problem.'

'What kind of a problem?'

'Well… seeing as we're now heading out of the system and I can't imagine any reason why we'd come ba—'

'Sorry,' interrupted Donna, jabbing a finger at him and wiggling it, pointedly. 'Heading out of the what?'

'The system – we've got what we need from there and now we're—'

'No, no. You're not listening: heading out of the *what*? The system?'

'The planetary system. We've broken orbit and now the *Dark Light* is en route to… to our next port of call.'

Donna took a couple of steps closer to him and drew herself up to her full height, which made Garaman look like a Munchkin.

'So, kidnapping me wasn't enough? Now you're flying me off to god-knows-where, leaving the Doctor behind?'

If it wasn't bad enough that she'd been separated from the Doctor, that separation was now getting greater by the minute.

'Is everyone from your planet quite so sharp?' asked Garaman. 'Only I'd hate to cross them, I really would. Where *are* you from?'

'It's called Earth, and you don't want to mess with us, you really don't.'

'Never heard of it. And what's so special about this Earth, then?'

'What's so special about it is that, if you pulled a kidnapping stunt like this back there you'd be in jail so fast that your feet wouldn't touch the ground.'

Garaman's eyes widened in mock fear.

'Oooh, you've got me trembling now! I'll have to make sure I don't cross these Earthons!'

'Humans,' corrected Donna. 'We're called humans.'

'How confusing. Delightfully quirky, but confusing. Now – the Doctor. Tell me about him.'

Donna folded her arms sullenly and clamped her lips shut, staring away into the middle distance pointedly. Garaman sighed, clicked his fingers at the bimbot standing in the corridor. Silently, it stepped into the room, its hands clasped formally in front of it.

'Start with her fingers,' Garaman said with the air of someone who had a hundred and one things to do and needed to start somewhere, just to get things moving. The robot reached out and, despite Donna's protestations and struggles, effortlessly raised her left hand. The skin of the machine was matt and smooth – skin-coloured but lacking any texture or veins. She felt sick as she realised what was going to happen.

'The little one first, I think,' Garaman said, turning away as if he really didn't want to witness the robot's next actions. 'Break it.'

THREE

The Doctor didn't bother banging on the cell door. They hadn't thought to take away his sonic screwdriver, and he knew he could probably be out of there in a couple of seconds. But he suspected that they'd put someone on guard outside: probably a robot, possibly even Mother. And whilst he reckoned that a quick blast from the screwdriver might be enough to scramble the brains of a robot, that seemed a bit of a drastic step, at least for now. Besides, if he tried anything like that, they'd have the sonic off him in seconds; and, just for now, he'd rather keep a hold of it.

The main thing, though, was that Boonie's ship was following Donna's. As long as they didn't lose it, he was happy to have a few minutes' quiet thinking time to himself.

The exhibit in the art gallery was definitely more than just a piece of art: there were some rather advanced resonance coils inside it, if the readings from the sonic screwdriver were anything to go by. He'd need to have a good poke about in it to work out what it was actually *for*, but if someone had gone to such lengths to steal it (and if Boonie and chums were at such pains to track it) then he suspected that it wasn't anything good. People didn't go to such efforts to steal – and track – the latest in toasters or hair-straighteners.

He glanced around the room they'd locked him in: it matched the rest of the ship – smelly, grimy and poky. If he'd been told he was on board a Second World War submarine, he'd have believed it. A rough bed with grubby blankets was in one corner and he wondered whether it belonged to one of the ship's crew. There were no knick-knacks or ornaments or other personal possessions about, so maybe they'd made up the guest bedroom specially for him. How kind.

A cup of tea would have gone down quite nicely round about now, too, although he didn't hold out much hope for room service.

It was a long time since the Doctor had been to the Andromeda galaxy, and he felt a little out of his depth: there was so much he didn't know about the civilisations here, which was one reason why he'd brought Donna. She'd been complaining that he always knew more about what was going on than she did, that it made her feel like a schoolgirl on a field trip with a particularly knowledgeable teacher. So he'd taken her somewhere that his own ignorance almost matched hers.

Maybe that had been a mistake.

He looked up as the door screeched open.

'Need some oil on that,' he muttered as an elderly

woman stepped silently into the room. In one hand there was a tray.

'Ah! Breakfast!' proclaimed the Doctor, jumping up. 'Now we're getting somewhere!'

'Stop!' barked a strange, musical voice.

Donna risked opening her eyes, half afraid that she'd open them just in time to see the robot snap the little finger that it now held so firmly in its cold grip. She felt her stomach clench.

'She's proving particularly intractable,' said Garaman peevishly. 'I thought that a little—'

'A little torture would help? Really, Garaman!'

The voice was coming from the doorway, but her view was blocked by the robot. Although it didn't release her, the pressure on her little finger lessened. She peered around the machine to see a particularly strange figure.

It looked a bit like something off *Walking With Dinosaurs*, except that it had three, thick legs, arranged like a tripod, a slim, upright body and three arms. Its head was a tall, oval shape with two wide, saucer-like deep blue eyes either side of a stumpy snout. The skin was lizardy, somehow, shading from grey at the top down through a beautiful, jewel-like turquoise across its chest and stomach down to an acid yellow at the feet. Slung across its shoulder was a broad belt with numerous pouches fastened to it. Other than that, it was naked. But then, it *was* a lizard.

'Torture doesn't work, Garaman,' said the creature, moving around so that Donna could see it properly. It walked oddly – well, perhaps not oddly, considering it had three legs – hopping from one leg to another, and then another. A bit like some injured insect. 'Torture someone and all they'll tell you is what they *think* you want to hear. What kind of animals are we if we have to resort to that?'

The creature looked Donna up and down with its huge, unblinking eyes, and one of its arms – the one sticking right out of the front of its chest – waved sinuously like a snake.

'This is not the way to treat organic-kind, Garaman. I am disappointed in you.'

'You've made your point,' hissed Garaman testily, waving the robot away from Donna. It dropped her arm instantly.

'Thank you,' said Donna, only then realising how she'd been holding her breath, waiting for the snap and the pain.

'Not at all,' said the lizard. You must be Donna. I'm Mesanth.'

It raised its front hand and spread its fingers – all three of them. It took Donna a few seconds to realise that this was some sort of handshake. But she was in no mood to be shaking hands with people who'd just tried to truncate one of her own.

'Where are you from?' asked Mesanth, lowering its hand when it realised Donna wasn't going to play nicely.

'Somewhere called Earth,' Garaman said. 'But she's simply called a "human".'

'Interesting,' said Mesanth, its voice somewhere between male and female. 'That word is generally used to mean bipedal, bilaterally symmetrical, mammalian organic-kind in our galaxy.'

'Bi-what?' asked Donna, still playing catch-up with the weird creature's words.

Mesanth's mouth twitched and it gestured at Garaman.

'Humans, you mean?' asked Donna, realising that Mesanth was talking about people like her and Garaman.

Mesanth gave an odd little chuckle from deep in its throat.

'Look, sunshine,' said Donna. 'Don't start getting all clever-clever, right? Just because you stopped this animal from…' Her voice tailed off as she was reminded of exactly what Mesanth had stopped Garaman from doing.

'Oh, please, no,' said Mesanth hastily. 'You misunderstand – I was not laughing at you. It is refreshing to get another perspective on ourselves. This Earth: where is it?'

'The Solar System,' said Donna through gritted teeth.

There was an awkward silence.

'And, erm, which solar system would that be? What is the name of its primary?'

'Its what?'

'Its star.'

'It's called…' Donna sighed, realising that, if these two thought she was a shilling short of a pound, she wasn't doing much to correct their impression. 'It's called the Sun.'

'How charming,' said Mesanth gently, like a slightly bemused posh aunt. 'The Sun.'

'You Earthons – humans,' interjected Garaman. 'Are you a newly emerged world?'

'A what?'

'Have you had much contact with other races in the galaxy?'

'Oh, loads,' Donna bluffed nonchalantly, not wanting to appear like some sort of backward country yokel. 'The Ood, the Magentans, the Racnoss, the… the lizard men of Wongo.' She shrugged casually. 'We're major players.'

'Never heard of any of them,' Garaman said sniffily.

'Well maybe you need to get out more,' Donna said. 'Besides,' she added, remembering what the Doctor had told her. 'Earth isn't even in this galaxy.'

Garaman's eyes widened almost imperceptibly.

'Really?'

'Really. Our galaxy is miles away.'

'Literally, I imagine.' This was Mesanth, sounding – again – as though it were laughing at her.

'Yes,' Donna retorted. 'Millions of them.'

She caught a glance between the two of them.

'Tell us more about your galaxy,' Mesanth said, its arms waving around sinuously like lizard's tongues. 'These lizard men of Wongo sound fascinating…'

The elderly woman that placed the tray down in front of the Doctor smiled tightly, apologetically.

'*The Sword of Justice* doesn't exactly excel at four-star cuisine, I'm afraid,' she said, gesturing to the bowl of swirly green soup and mug of insipid tea. 'Li'ian,' she added, raising her palm. The Doctor matched it. She had long, grey hair tied up in a complicated knot on the top of her head and big, blue eyes. Sharp, intelligent eyes, thought the Doctor.

The Sword of Justice, eh? Bit of a pompous name for a ship, isn't it?'

'That's Boonie for you,' Li'ian smiled.

'I'd rather gathered that he could do with a sense of humour transplant. I'm the Doctor,' he smiled, 'but you probably know that already.'

'Boonie told me. He can be a bit severe, but he's not a bad sort.'

'Rather young for commanding a ship, isn't he?' The Doctor took a sip of the tea and pulled a face.

'Oh, he's not as young as he looks – his race age slower than the rest of us. Sadly. He's in his forties, believe it or not.' Li'ian gave a little, twinkly smile. 'I should find out what they put in the water on his planet, shouldn't I?'

'And what planet would that be?'

'He's from Dallendaf.'

'Ah,' said the Doctor, none-the-wiser. 'And you?'

'Born on Poopop, grew up all over the place.'

'You're kidding!' exclaimed the Doctor with a grin.

'You know it?'

'Nope – but isn't it marvellous that there's a planet called *Poopop*! Anyway, what's all this about, Li'ian – this little mission of yours. You're not art thieves but you're following someone who is. Not police, not with a ship and crew like this – no offence.'

Li'ian shook her head sadly.

'That's up to Boonie to tell you. But we're more interested in you.'

'Really? Should I be flattered or alarmed?'

'You appear from nowhere and just happen to be around

when the exhibit is stolen. And your friend just happens to be stolen along with it.' She raised an eyebrow. 'A bit of a coincidence, wouldn't you say?'

'I like to think of it as the universe making sure I'm in the right place at the right time. It has a habit of doing that.'

'And you claim to know nothing about what the exhibit is.'

'Other than it being not just an exhibit at all?'

Li'ian paused.

'Boonie wants to speak to you.'

'Does he indeed? Well, I'm always up for a nice chat.' He glanced around his room. 'My place – or his?'

Donna knew that she wasn't exactly wowing Mesanth and Garaman with her knowledge of the Earth's galaxy. Short of naming a few of the planets she'd been to, and throwing in a bit of stuff the Doctor had told her (which, on reflection, she was sure she'd got half wrong) there wasn't a great deal she seemed to be able to do to impress the two of them. But the important thing at the moment was to keep on their good sides, to make sure they didn't decide she was a waste of oxygen and chuck her out of the airlock. She hoped that the Doctor was on her tail – she knew that he'd be doing all he could to find her, so all she had to do was to make sure that she was still alive when he finally did.

Her kidnappers listened attentively, asked a few questions, but, ultimately, seemed a bit disappointed. She wasn't sure what, exactly, they were after. Maybe, as they claimed, they were just curious. But she kept an eye on

Garaman: after the stunt with her finger, she was in no mood to start trusting him just yet.

The door hissed open suddenly, just as she was trying to explain about the Jant and their plan to hollow out Callisto, and a robot appeared. This time, it wasn't one of the supermodels, but a much smaller one: milky-white and about the height of a small child, it had a weird-looking row of four tiny hands jutting from its chest and a featureless, spherical head. It made a weird, giggly noise.

Garaman must have noticed her discomfort.

'Not a fan of mechanicals?' he said with a smile.

'Give me a video recorder or an mp3 player and I'm fine – it's just…' She waved in the direction of the little robot. 'Well, don't you think they're a bit *creepy*?'

Garaman's eyes flicked up to Mesanth's.

'Mechanicals are just tools,' he said reassuringly. Then he turned to the robot. 'What?' he barked, and Donna winced slightly.

'Ogmunee wishes me to tell you that we will arrive in the system in one hour,' said the thing in a fluting, childlike voice

Garaman ignored the robot and then, when it didn't move, he motioned it away with a sharp gesture. The little thing toddled off.

'Do they…' ventured Donna. 'Are they…? I mean, do they think? Like us, I mean.'

'Like organics?' asked Mesanth. 'Not really. They can ape – if you'll pardon the expression – organic behaviour and responses, but it's all just programmed, regardless of what the promechanicals would have you believe.'

'The promechanicals?'

'The trendy thinking-classes who go on about mechanicals having rights, feelings, that sort of nonsense.' Mesanth paused and leaned closer to Donna. She could smell something like lavender and fish. 'Do you have mechanicals in your galaxy, on your world?'

Donna rolled her eyes.

'Don't get me started,' she said. 'Robot Santas! I mean, how wrong is *that*? I was kidnapped by one – took me off in a taxi. On my wedding day! Can you believe it? And the robots on Planet 1 – they were just weird.'

Garaman nodded sagely.

'It seems that even in your galaxy, things are the same.'

'It's in their nature,' said Mesanth with a sorrowful shake of the head. 'Our scientists proved it decades ago: mechanicals are unable to think or feel the same way that organics do. It's the way they're made. Not their fault, but true nonetheless.'

Donna nodded. From the bits the Doctor had told her about his previous trips, robots were bad news. And the ones she'd met here hadn't exactly endeared themselves to her.

'It seems,' said Garaman, warming to her, 'that we have more in common than we might have imagined. Perhaps,' he paused and glanced at Mesanth, 'we should be a little more hospitable to Donna. Apologies for my earlier actions. Perhaps, when you understand the *Dark Light*'s mission, you might find it in your heart to forgive me.' Garaman smiled tightly, but Donna didn't reciprocate. The man had a lot of forgiveness to earn yet.

'Perhaps, as a small gesture, you might like a guided tour of the ship?'

As apologies for threatening to break a finger, it was a bit limp. But it was a start. And it would give her a chance to find out more about her kidnappers.

FOUR

The control room of *The Sword of Justice* was a hive of activity as Li'ian ushered the Doctor in. Mother was nowhere to be seen, but Kellique and Boonie were hunched over the sensor displays. Three or four robots of assorted – and bizarre – design were scuttling around, like shiny, hyper-trendy kitchen gadgets. The ship groaned and creaked unnervingly.

'Doctor,' said Boonie, catching sight of him. 'We're just about to arrive in the Karris system.'

'Are we?' enthused the Doctor. 'Marvellous. Where's that, then?'

'Sorry – I forgot that you're not familiar with our galaxy.'

'Well, there're a lot of galaxies out there, Boonie. Have to spread myself about a bit.' He squeezed in between Boonie and Kellique and peered down at the sensor display. 'So what's so special about this Karris system, then?'

'It's where the cultist ship is.'

'The cultist ship? Oh, you mean Donna's ship! Why d'you call it "the cultist ship", then?'

There was another of those looks between Kellique and Boonie.

'Oh, come on!' exclaimed the Doctor. 'You can't keep talking in riddles like this. Imagine if we all did: "I think I'd like a... you know... one of those bowls with a handle on it. Full of that stuff. Liquid. Warm."' He let his shoulders sag. 'We'd be here for ever at that rate.'

'I'm sorry, Doctor, but you've been on our ship barely two hours. Until we know whether we can trust you, I think it's better that we play our cards close to our chests.'

The Doctor shrugged.

'Fair enough, but Li'ian thought that maybe it was time we were all a bit more communicative.'

Boonie threw Li'ian a glance, which she returned.

'It's true,' she said, holding her ground. 'The Doctor might have been dragged into this accidentally, as he claims. Or... or he might not. He's certainly not as stupid as he looks.'

'Go on,' said the Doctor to Boonie. 'Say it: "No one could be as stupid as *he* looks." Believe me, I've heard it before. Don't judge a book by its cover. Now why don't you just tell me what you're up to, and I can decide whether to help you or to stop you.' He beamed brightly at them.

The three Andromedans exchanged silent glances before Boonie finally nodded.

'Li'ian might have a point.'

He straightened up and walked over to his command chair, beckoning the Doctor.

'What d'you know about the Cult of Shining Darkness?'

'Good name for a band?' He pulled a thoughtful face. 'Something a bit rocky, a bit glam. An album band,' he decided. 'Not much good for singles. Getting close?'

Boonie sighed.

'What you said about no one being as stupid as you look…'

The Doctor grinned back. 'OK, OK – this Cult of Shining Darkness. Never heard of them. What do they do?'

'Until a few years ago,' Boonie said, his voice low and deadly serious, 'they were nothing but a bunch of cranks. Cranks with money and brains, but still cranks.'

'And since then?'

'Since then – since the death of their leader, a woman called Khnu em Llodis – they've been quiet. Until two months ago, that is.'

'And then they resurfaced?'

Boonie nodded.

'So what exactly does this cult believe in? I mean, cults normally believe in something don't they, even if it's complete nonsense – and it usually is. Part of the job description.'

The Doctor noticed how Boonie glanced at Kellique and Li'ian, who were following the conversation from the sensor control panel.

'They're organic supremacists.'

'Meaning they're not too hot on robots?'

Boonie winced slightly. 'The correct term – well, the *most* correct term – is machine intelligences, Doctor. The cultists call them "mechanicals" which should give you some idea of how they think.'

'So "robots" is bad, then?'

Boonie winced again.

'Unless you're talking about non-sentient appliances, yes, generally. Any that rates higher than a forty on the Lipanov scale is a machine intelligence.' He rolled his eyes. 'Although you ask a dozen machine intelligences and you'll get a dozen different answers. Some prefer "designed organisms", some prefer "non-organics".' He shook his head and gave a tired grin. 'It can be a minefield at times.'

It was the Doctor's turn to smile wryly.

'You know, wherever I go in the universe it's the same.' He gave a shrug. 'Still, it's all about courtesy, isn't it? If a vending machine wants to be called "Barbara", it'd be rude to call it anything else.'

'Exactly! And believe me, if the cultists got their way, every machine intelligence would be nothing but a "mechanical". They wouldn't even rate a name like – what was it? – Barbara.'

The Doctor nodded and rubbed the back of his neck.

'So: cultists not too hot on sentient rights for all, then?'

'They refuse to believe that machine intelligences *are* sentient. They consider them as tools mimicking sentient behaviour. Despite all the evidence, they see anything non-organic as nothing but a collection of parts.'

'And what does Mother have to say about this Cult of Shining Darkness?' He glanced around the room. 'I notice she's not here. Busy?'

'Mother keeps herself to herself a lot of the time. She's

not the Cult's greatest fan, as you can imagine.'

'And you lot,' the Doctor said, glancing around the room. 'You're on a mission to track the Cult down? Why?'

'Because,' said Kellique from the other side of the room, 'they have to be stopped.'

The Doctor frowned. 'Stopped? Stopped from doing what?'

Boonie shook his head.

'That's what we're trying to work out.'

Suddenly, Kellique let out a little cry of surprise. Before anyone could stop him, the Doctor was at her side, peering at the sensor displays.

'It's gone!' said the woman, her hands flying frantically over the controls.

'Hyperjumped out of the system?' the Doctor muttered, gently elbowing her out of the way. He shook his head. 'No, there'd be a residual trace, even if just for a few seconds – hold this, will you?'

He'd stripped down to his shirt sleeves and was holding his jacket out for Kellique. Silently, and still somewhat shocked, she took it as he began to mess with the controls.

'Doctor!' barked Boonie. 'What are you doing?'

'I'm trying,' said the Doctor, pulling out the access panel in the base of the controls, rolling onto his back and sticking his head inside, 'to boost your sensors. Judging by the last few seconds of your sensor log, your little culty friends have just switched their shields into overdrive.'

'Which means?'

'Which means,' said the Doctor through gritted teeth

as he tugged at the circuit boards and crystals, rewiring them, 'that whatever they're doing, they're rather keen to make sure that no one else knows about it.'

Seconds later he emerged, sprang to his feet and set about fiddling with the sensor controls again.

'There!' he cried triumphantly. 'Got 'em!'

Garaman's ship was, Donna decided (on the basis of the few spaceships she'd seen so far) decidedly palatial. Spotlessly clean (due, no doubt, to the oodles of little robots running around, polishing everything to within an inch of its life). Garaman had other things to deal with, so Mesanth had offered to show Donna around. Which, considering the finger incident, suited her fine.

Mesanth was quite the opposite of the slimy little man – gracious and entertaining and (appearance aside) not the least bit threatening. She was still getting used to the creature's odd, bouncing walk (and still hadn't summoned up the courage to ask whether Mesanth was male or female, so she decided to plump for male, just on the basis of 'his' voice) but managed to keep up with him well enough. Her thoughts, though, were still on the Doctor, and how they were going to get her back to him. She'd brought it up with Mesanth as he'd given her a quick look in the ship's engine room. (If she'd needed any evidence about Mesanth's gender, that ought to have clinched it: what woman, thought Donna as she tried to look interested, would have suggested a trip round an *engine room*, for god's sake?)

'It's tricky,' said Mesanth, leading her back out into the corridor where a creature a little like a huge armadillo trundled past, flicking its tail in a sort-of-wave at them. 'Our… our *mission* is of the utmost importance to us,' Mesanth said in that slightly haughty way of his.

'And getting back to the Doctor is of the utmost importance to me. Can't you just send him a message? Tell him I'm here?'

'Garaman would never allow it, I'm afraid. But look at it this way: this Doctor friend of yours – he's not going to leave the planet without you, is he?'

'He wouldn't dare!'

'Well there you are: he'll wait until we return you to him.'

'And when, exactly, will that be?' Donna stopped dead in the corridor and one of the little cleaning robots – a chrome dome like those things that cover your food up in posh restaurants – made a little detour around her feet. 'Only I don't exactly get a sense of urgency about it. And what if the Doctor thinks I'm dead, or gone for ever? How long's he going to wait before he decides I'm not coming back?'

Mesanth shrugged with his two side arms which just made Donna want to punch him.

'What can I say? Apart from Garaman's, um, unfortunate outburst earlier, I don't believe we're treating you badly—'

'You're keeping me prisoner on a ship that's going in the wrong direction!' exploded Donna. 'Your boss almost broke off my finger! It's a pretty twisted idea of not treating someone badly!'

A pale, haughty-looking woman in overalls was just coming out of the control room as Donna finished her tirade, and gave her an awkward smile. Donna just grimaced at her. In the control room, Garaman was in a huddle with two other humans. They abruptly stopped talking as Donna and Mesanth entered.

'We've picked up the ship,' said Garaman to Mesanth, eyeing Donna.

'In the system?' Mesanth danced over to Garaman and cast his eyes over the instruments.

'Entering it. Behind us.'

Mesanth's gaze snapped up to Garaman.

'It's them,' Mesanth said crisply.

'As long as we're sure it's them,' said one of the other humans – a bald man with ridiculously muscled arms and skin the colour of dark mahogany. 'If it's anyone else, we might be in trouble. Has she been checked for homing devices, tags?' He stared at Donna. And not in a good way.

Mesanth nodded.

For a moment – for one silly, heart-stopping moment – Donna imagined that maybe the Doctor had found out who'd kidnapped her and was riding to her rescue. She realised she was smiling when the muscled guy frowned at her.

'What's so funny?' he barked.

'Nothing,' said Donna defensively.

Mesanth turned towards her, his huge eyes wide and unblinking.

'You're thinking that this is your friend, the Doctor, coming to rescue you?' he asked.

The tone of Mesanth's voice suggested that he knew something she didn't. If it *wasn't* the Doctor…

'Could be,' she said, trying to sound as positive as possible.

'Could be,' said Garaman. 'But isn't.' He smiled tightly. 'Sorry.'

'So who is it then, Mr Know-It-All?'

Garaman folded his arms and gave her a smug look.

'Just a minor annoyance,' he said. 'But you know what they say: keep your friends close and your enemies even closer. As long as we know where they are and what they're doing, they're fine. Sadly for you, though, it's not this Doctor person.'

Donna's heart sank.

Wherever he went, the Doctor thought, it was the same old story, wasn't it? One group of intelligent beings (whether they were robots, humans, multidimensional entities living in a fold in space-time or whatever) decided that another group didn't qualify for basic rights, human or otherwise. Sometimes it was based on biology; sometimes on culture or religion or on whether they preferred eating trifle with a spoon or a fork. But what always followed was persecution, war and death. Lots of death. And no matter how advanced or civilised they were, they always managed to justify it. To themselves, if not to anyone else.

'I don't know what you did,' said Boonie, breaking him out of his reverie, 'but the range of our sensors, never mind their sensitivity, has almost doubled.' He narrowed his eyes and stared at him. 'Just who are you?'

'I've told you – I'm the Doctor.'

'That's not a name – it's a job title.'

'Well, as long as I get the job done, isn't it enough?'

Boonie gave him a thoughtful look. 'For now, maybe.'

'A little thank you wouldn't go amiss, either.'

'Thank you,' said Boonie, almost reluctantly. 'But I'm still not convinced that you're on our side.'

'Oh, believe me,' said the Doctor. '*I'm* not sure whose side I'm on yet, so that probably makes us even. But if you want any more of my help, you're going to have to trust me. Tell me about this Karris system.'

Boonie thought for a moment and nodded.

'According to the database,' Boonie said, tapping at the controls and bringing up a set of whizzy-looking graphics, 'it's not a particularly interesting system: a red giant sun, two gas planets and a small, human-suitable planet. According to records, it was once quite a nice place, but solar flares have turned it into something of a desert.'

'Natives?'

'Primitive ape-like creatures called the Jaftee are at the top of the evolutionary ladder here – simple tool-makers, builders. No advanced technology.'

'So why d'you think the Cult have stopped over here?'

'Could be a way of trying to shake us off,' Boonie suggested.

'And if they think they're still shielded,' the Doctor said, 'then they should be on their way pretty soon.'

'Would make sense,' Boonie agreed.

The Doctor gave a great big stretch.

'So while we wait to see if they do, why don't you tell me a bit more about this Khnu em Llodis woman? With a name like that, I'm sure she has an interesting story.'

***

As the snowy glare of the transmat field faded, the blood-red light of Karris's sun washed over everything. Donna's skin began to tingle, and she realised it was because of the constant slew of sand grains, battering against her in the wind. The air smelled dry and dead, of heat and of the flinty tang of the sand.

'Ahhhh…'

It was Mesanth, standing by her side and letting out a sigh of what Donna realised was relief.

'Ahhh?' she muttered, squinting to keep the sandstorm out of her eyes.

'Smells like home,' explained Mesanth, flexing his fingers like a cat kneading a woolly jumper. 'Bliss!'

'Smells of death,' muttered Ogmunee, the muscled guy that had given her such dirty looks aboard the ship. He stood alongside her, at his back one of the bimbots, cold and impassive and silent.

'Well before you start trying to sell me a timeshare here,' said Donna, casting around for somewhere to shelter from the relentless sandstorm that threatened to scour her skin down to the bone, 'can we at least get under cover? Assuming there is some cover. I'm beginning to wish I'd brought my coat.'

She squinted, sheltering her eyes, and scanned the surface of Karris. Clear to the horizon, in every direction, was nothing but flat, orange sand. It was like Norfolk, only blisteringly hot.

She turned back to see Mesanth skipping away across the sand, some sort of device in his hand bleeping and twittering. Ogmunee scowled at her and followed him, the robot at his tail.

'So where's this segment thing, then?' Donna gasped, racing to catch up with them. Ogmunee pointed downwards.

'So why not just beam us straight down there, then? Giving us the scenic tour, are you?'

'Too risky,' said Ogmunee laconically. 'The sandstorms are generating too much electrostatic interference for us to be sure that we'd materialise at all. And we haven't mapped the tunnels yet.'

'Oooh!' said Donna sourly, pushing back her hair as it whipped around her. 'Tunnels! You know how to spoil a girl, don't you?'

'Why did we bring her?' Ogmunee asked Mesanth tiredly as the creature rotated on the spot, scanning the ground beneath them with his squeaking device.

'Despite what Garaman thinks,' Mesanth said, 'I believe that Donna has more in common with us than she might believe. It's only courteous to include her in our... activities.'

Ogmunee just grumped and scowled at Donna – who wasn't sure she swallowed Mesanth's explanation. She wondered if it were more to keep Donna out of Garaman's face. Suited her fine.

'She's more likely to be a liability than an asset. Garaman's losing his mind,' he said.

A second later, Mesanth let out a little hiss. 'Ah!' he exclaimed. 'The entrance! About five metres this way.'

And off the three-legged lizard went, Donna and

Ogmunee and the robot in hot pursuit. Mesanth paused a few seconds later at what looked like nothing more than a flattish, sand-coloured rock lying on the ground. In the midst of the sandstorm around them it was almost invisible. He pushed at it with one of his feet and it slid effortlessly aside, rotating as if pivoted at one corner.

'You're stronger than you look,' Donna said, casting a sidelong glance at Ogmunee. 'Should've got Mr Muscles here to do it.'

'No strength involved,' said Mesanth, slipping the scanner into one of the pouches of his shoulder belt. 'It's counterbalanced.'

As the rock continued to swing out of the way, Donna saw a flight of rough-hewn steps, the colour of the sand, descending into the darkness. With a glance at her and Ogmunee, Mesanth stepped down into the shadows.

FIVE

Khnu em Llodis had been a genius. Well, that's what she told everyone. And from what the Doctor gathered, it sounded like pretty much everyone believed her.

'One of our greatest roboticists,' Li'ian said as the Doctor scanned the scrolling display in front of him.

She'd taken him to the ship's 'library' (little more than a storeroom with some rickety shelves and a desk) and shown him dozens of documents and transcripts relating to Khnu, stretching over more than a decade, when the scientist had been at her height.

'So what went wrong?'

He spun in his seat to face Li'ian. She shrugged.

'Some say she just went mad.'

'Happens a lot,' the Doctor agreed. 'Scientists. Always going mad. Especially the top-class ones.' He paused and looked up at Li'ian. 'You never hear of the second-rate ones going mad, though, do you? Always the geniuses. Funny, that.'

'Some say she discovered a truth that threatened the entire galaxy.'

'That'll be what she meant by this bit, then,' he said, turning back to the display and reading aloud. '"But there is a dark heart to our shining empire, a dark heart that, until now, we have chosen to ignore. A dark heart that, if not addressed, will rise up and destroy all that we have built."' He spun back to face Li'ian. 'What d'you reckon she meant by that?'

Li'ian nodded thoughtfully and folded her hands on her lap. 'Everyone assumed that she was talking about machine intelligences,' she said simply. 'That speech was the last one she ever gave. En route back to her own planet, after the conference, her ship was destroyed.'

'*Mysteriously* destroyed,' corrected the Doctor, pointing to the screen.

'*Mysteriously* destroyed,' agreed Li'ian. 'There were rumours that she was killed because she was speaking the truth.'

'Well,' said the Doctor. 'It's a very flexible thing, the truth, isn't it?'

'Not for her,' Li'ian said. 'For Khnu, it was always very clear. Very black and white.'

The Doctor took a deep breath.

'Anyway,' he said. 'Enough of the official documents. What do *you* think?'

'Me?' Li'ian seemed surprised.

'You're aboard a ship, tracking people who – I assume – think like Khnu did. This Cult of Shining Darkness. They've stolen a whopping great lump of technology from an art gallery, and now they've stopped off at a planet that doesn't seem to have much more going for it than Lanzarote. And you're still following them. You must have some idea of what they're doing.'

Li'ian took a breath and glanced around the empty library room as if she thought she might be being overheard.

'Boonie will probably have me raked over the coals for this,' she said eventually, chewing on her bottom lip. 'But we think they're collecting the parts of something. Some sort of device or maybe some sort of map.'

'Really?' The Doctor was all ears.

'When Khnu was killed – when she died, whatever – her little band of followers went quiet for two years. Most of them just disappeared. Possibly killed by whoever killed Khnu. But then rumours began to circulate that she'd been working on something before her death – something connected with her research field.'

'Robotics?'

'Robotics. Despite being a genius in artificial intelligence, Khnu refused to believe that machine intelligences, mechanicals, whatever you want to call them, were truly intelligent. Her speech, thinly veiled as it was, was aimed at those who considered machines intelligences to be on a par with organic ones. She believed that they simply mimicked intelligence, and that the organic races of the galaxy had fallen for it, hook, line and sinker. It's reported that she foresaw a time when the galaxy's machine races would rise up against the organics and slaughter us all.'

'That's what she meant by "the darkness"?'

'That's what they say. And the rumours are that these things they're collecting have something to do with it.'

The Doctor rubbed the back of his neck.

'Interesting.' He paused and stared thoughtfully into the distance. 'So these artefacts – part of a device, or a locator or something maybe? Like one of those partwork magazines: "Builds week by week into the ultimate robot defence"? How many instalments are we talking? A little one like *Delia's How To Boil Water* or a whopper like *The Star Trek Files?*'

'Sorry?'

The Doctor grinned.

'D'you reckon the cultists have got all the bits already, or are they going to be searching for ever?'

'Your guess is as good as mine, Doctor. All we know – all we *believe*,' Li'ian corrected herself, 'is that when Khnu died, the Cult went into a panic and scattered the pieces of the thing around the galaxy, scared that robot sympathisers would find them and destroy them.'

'Ahhh…' The Doctor smiled. 'That's why you didn't want to go barging in, isn't it? *You* lot want them to find all the bits, put it together, and *then* you can go barging in and collect the whole set, ringbinders and all!'

'Ringbinders?'

He waved his hand.

'Don't worry about it.' He leaped out of his seat suddenly, making Li'ian flinch. 'Right! Let's get this party started!'

And before Li'ian could stop him he was halfway to the door.

***

'Thanks for not telling me to bring a cardy,' Donna muttered as the rock above them swung back into place, cutting out not only the drizzling sand and the gusting wind but the searing heat of the red sun. It suddenly felt cold and clammy. Mesanth produced a torch from his shoulder belt and flicked it on, illuminating broad, sand-silted steps leading down into the Stygian darkness.

'You humans are remarkably susceptible to changes in environmental temperature, aren't you?' he said over his shoulder as he began the descent.

'*Some* humans,' grunted Ogmunee from behind Donna.

'At least some of us have the decency not to go around half-naked,' muttered Donna. 'Anyway, what's this segment thing look like?'

'You've already seen the second one – the artefact from the gallery.'

'Oh, that! Right. So we're looking for another one of those, are we? Shouldn't be hard to spot. And why's it here?'

'Safekeeping,' said Mesanth cryptically, and then fell into silence as, out of the darkness beneath them, came a hideous roar that echoed on and on and on.

Donna took a deep breath. 'That sounds *very* safe.'

'You said this place smells of home,' Donna whispered as they descended. 'Where's that, then?'

'It's called Lota. Lovely planet – dry, dusty.' Mesanth gave a little sigh.

'So how come you got mixed up with Garaman?'

'I worked with one of his associates a few years ago. She... introduced me to Garaman and Ogmunee here and the others. She offered me a job.'

'Headhunted, eh? Better than temping, I bet. What kind of work?'

'Are you always this full of questions?' grunted Ogmunee from behind her.

'Only when no one's bothering to give me answers, yes. Why? Got a problem with that? Something to hide, maybe?'

'Stop it!' warbled Mesanth.

'You don't like conflict, do you?' asked Donna as the stairs began to curve around to the right.

'The Lotapareen have evolved from highly communal herbivorous ancestors: violence and conflict are alien to us.'

'Must make all this adventuring a bit of a nightmare.'

'Mesanth knows what has to be done,' came Ogmunee's voice again.

'And what is that, exactly?'

No one answered her. Abruptly, the steps ended and Mesanth's torch beam revealed that they were in some sort of antechamber, blank stone surrounding them. As the ellipse of light from the torch flitted about the walls, Donna caught sight of something.

'What's that?' she asked, taking the torch from him.

Most of the wall was taken up with a primitive, scribbled drawing of a huge, tentacled mass with a single, monstrous eye and a slavering mouth. And, to give some sense of scale, four of its tentacles held what looked like squat little stick figures. One of them was being thrust into the toothy mouth.

'Tell me that this isn't one of those "Beware of the dog" signs,' she said.

'The Jaftee probably worship this creature as a god,' said Mesanth with a vague air of fascination.

'The Jaftee?'

'The inhabitants of Karris. Primitive ape-like creatures. No offence,' he added with a sidelong glance at Donna.

'None taken – I think.'

'We don't anticipate any problems with the Jaftee,' Ogmunee said. 'We seeded their culture years ago. They should see us as even greater gods than this thing.'

'So,' said Donna, handing Mesanth his torch. 'Not too bright, then, these Jaftee.'

'Simple creatures,' agreed Mesanth, scanning the wall in front of them and running his two spare hands over its surface. 'Ah!'

At this exclamation, there was a dull clunk and the three-legged creature stepped back. A deep, teeth-aching grinding noise started up and the chamber around them began to vibrate. Little whorls of sand drifted down in the torch's path as a segment of the wall swung back and away.

'So why the robot?' she asked Mesanth as they set off deeper into the bowels of the planet. 'You said you had these Jaftee people trained to think you're gods.'

'Insurance,' said Mesanth simply, and Donna saw his huge eyes dart briefly to the wall painting of the tentacled thing. If the little stick figures being crammed into its dribbling mouth were even vaguely human-sized, she wasn't sure that a robot – even one as strong and silent as the one they'd brought along – would be enough to fight it off.

'I don't know what you did to the sensors, Doctor, but we've actually managed to pick up a signal from beneath Karris's surface.'

Kellique smiled appreciatively as the Doctor and Li'ian entered the control room. Boonie was nowhere to be seen.

'Marvellous! Picked up what?'

Kellique gestured for him to come and look.

'Hmmm…' said the Doctor thoughtfully. 'If I didn't know any better – and obviously I do, otherwise I wouldn't be saying this – I'd swear that that's a similar energy profile to the segment that they stole from the art gallery. And this other signal – here – looks like the same transmat energy signature that whisked Donna and the segment up to the Cult's ship.'

Kellique nodded – and did a double-take, before throwing a sharp look at Li'ian. The Doctor noticed and gave a gentle shrug.

'Li'ian here told me all about Khnu and her little band of followers.'

'Oh…' said Kellique, looking a little worried. 'Boonie's going to be pleased about that.'

'Pleased about what?'

They all turned at the sound of Boonie's voice: he stood in the doorway, his face hard and angry.

Li'ian stepped forwards.

'I told him about Khnu and about what we think the Cult are up to.'

'You did *what*?!' exploded Boonie.

'Oh, don't blame Li'ian—' began the Doctor, but Boonie cut him off with a wave of the hand.

'Boonie!' snapped Kellique. 'We were the ones that brought him on board, remember? And his modifications to our sensors are amazing: come here and look. We've picked up similar readings to those from the second segment from the gallery.'

Boonie was speechless; and, although he glared at the Doctor, he said nothing and went to check the readings.

'So this is the *third* part?' the Doctor said. 'Still no idea how many of them there are? I mean, I know I've got a fairly long lifespan, but I wouldn't want to think I'll be chasing around the universe for the next forty years, looking for the other bits.'

'Yes,' said Kellique, keeping an eye on Boonie for his reaction, 'we think this is the third one. The second one was in the gallery and the first was hidden in a forest on Chao.'

Boonie just glared.

'Hmmm,' the Doctor mused. 'Shame I didn't get a chance to have a proper look at the second one. I might have been able to work out exactly what the finished thing's supposed to do.' He paused. 'But now that my little modifications have let you find the third one, why don't we use your matter transmitter to pop down and take a look before they beam it away?'

He stared at them all, eyebrows raised expectantly.

'I mean,' he added, shoving his hands into his pockets, 'I know you're waiting for them to collect the whole set before you swoop in, but if we were to just take a teensy little peek at it… Not take it; just a little look-see…'

It was clear from Kellique's expression that she didn't think the idea was a bad one at all, but Li'ian shook her head.

'The Cultists have been in orbit almost an hour already. They won't waste time. That transmat trace means they've already sent a recovery team down – there's too much electrostatic interference in Karris's atmosphere for them to beam it out directly without using a signal booster like they did from the art gallery. They can just about make it to the planet's surface, but from there they'll be on foot.'

'Well,' said the Doctor, studying the floor thoughtfully and casually. 'If you let me have a go at your transmat, you never know: I might be able to boost it like I did with your sensors. And then we could beam in, check it out, and then be gone before they even know we've been…'

All eyes were on Boonie: as the head of this rag-tag mission, they clearly all deferred to him. Most of the time, anyway.

The Doctor grinned wolfishly.

'Don't tell me you wouldn't like to know what they're up to. And who knows? If we can work out what this thing does, before they've assembled it, you'll have even more chance of stopping them from using it.' He held Boonie's gaze. 'Go on! Live a little!'

***

Donna flinched – and, to her shame, grabbed hold of Mesanth – as another howling roar echoed out of the darkness ahead of them.

'This thing,' she said slowly. 'This creature. What exactly do you know about it? I mean, you said you'd been here before and ponced about dressed up as gods or something, right? So, you actually saw it, right?'

Mesanth's eyes glinted in the torchlight.

'Not… as such.'

Donna rolled her eyes.

'So for all you know, it could be waiting around the next corner to stuff us into its mouth – y'know, like on that mural back there.'

'The robot will protect us,' said Ogmunee. Donna peered over his shoulder to where the slender, blonde thing stood silently, its face cold and impassive.

'No offence, Mr Muscles, but you're out of your tree if you think that she – it – can fight off something the size of that creature.'

'And I have this,' said Ogmunee, holding up a slender, silver tube. 'A thermal projector.'

Donna relaxed a little. 'That a fancy term for a space gun?'

Mesanth said nothing, but Donna could tell from the way he glanced at Ogmunee's gun that he wasn't impressed.

'Wouldn't it be an idea if blondie went first?' Donna added after a moment's thought, indicating the robot.

Mesanth considered Donna's suggestion and agreed, waving the silent robot forwards.

'Your type, then, is she?' Donna whispered to Ogmunee

as the robot took up position at the front. 'Strong and silent.'

Ogmunee opened his mouth to say something, but was cut off by another roar – a roar that sounded distinctly closer than the last one had done.

Mesanth took a couple of steps back, allowing Ogmunee forwards, just behind the robot.

What happened in the next few seconds, Donna wasn't quite sure. A horrendous howl shattered the clammy silence of the tunnel and something huge and dark surged out of the side of the passage, striking the bimbot and slamming it up against the opposite wall with a screech of metal and a crash that echoed away into the blackness.

Ogmunee jumped back, his torch skittering away across the floor like some mad, terrified firefly. He bumped into Donna who fell back against Mesanth.

As her eyes tried to adjust to the darkness, Donna saw faint sparkles of light come from the robot as part of its face fell away, clattering to the ground.

'Back! Back!' cried Mesanth, whirling on his three feet and pushing Donna away, leaving Ogmunee at the front.

'Use your gun!' shouted Donna as, dimly, she saw thrashing tentacles oozing out into the passage.

Suddenly, the roaring subsided, and, glancing past Ogmunee, Donna saw that the creature's tentacles had vanished back into the opening in the tunnel. Sprawled on the floor, its spine snapped and folded back on itself, was the robot. A few more crackles of light danced within the circuitry of its head as it turned towards them. Despite the fact that it was a robot, Donna felt vaguely sick. It was the movement of the head that made her act.

'Help it!' she cried.

She looked at Mesanth, to see that he was staring at her in disbelief.

'Help it!' she said again, her voice lower and more angry, now that the lizard man seemed to be ignoring her.

'It's a robot,' grunted Ogmunee swinging the beam from his torch over it.

'It's *injured*,' Donna said, unable to believe their lack of concern.

'It's damaged,' corrected Ogmunee.

Donna just glared at him.

'Keep your eye out for that thing,' she said. 'And your gun for that matter.'

And before anyone could stop her, she crept forwards, keeping her back to the wall against which the broken robot lay. Something inside it whirred pitifully.

'It's OK,' Donna said quietly, risking a quick glance down at it. 'You'll be OK.'

'What is she doing?' she heard Ogmunee whisper, disbelievingly, to Mesanth.

'I'm trying to help it,' she answered, trying to keep the fear out of her own voice. At any second, the creature could be back. She checked that Ogmunee was keeping her back covered.

'How are you?' Donna whispered to the robot, realising that this could well be the bimbot that Garaman had instructed to break her finger. Strangely, it didn't seem to matter. 'You're going soft,' she whispered to herself as it clicked and sparked pathetically and raised a shuddering arm towards her.

For a moment, everything was silent – and then, unmistakeably, Donna heard the sound of the creature in the darkness, a deep, stomach-churning roar. She leaped to her feet and backed away, pushing Ogmunee and Mesanth behind her. Something dark and sinuous flicked out of the tunnel towards them, smacking against the wall and sending little puffs of dust into the air.

'Move!' she cried, wishing that Ogmunee would use his gun. She felt the breeze from one of the creature's tentacles as it thrashed about, briefly catching the light from Mesanth's torch.

'Shoot it!' Donna called as Ogmunee pushed alongside her and raised his arm. Glancing down, she saw the tip of his weapon glow a deep cherry red and there was a ferocious howl from up ahead.

'You've hurt it!' cried Mesanth.

'Well, d'uh!' shouted Donna. 'That is rather the point!'

Ogmunee fired again, and they heard the creature roar in pain.

'Keep firing,' Donna said.

'Maybe we've hurt it enough,' whimpered Mesanth.

'Not as long as we can still hear it, we haven't.'

'I don't like this,' Mesanth said, and Donna could hear the distress in his voice.

The tentacled thing seemed to have gone quiet, though whether it was dead or just licking its wounds, Donna wasn't certain.

'Isn't there another way through?' Donna asked Mesanth, who started fiddling with his scanner. The cold light lit up his face from below, and she could see his lips trembling.

'This is the only way through,' he said. 'That creature is obviously a guard dog.'

'So we either go on and try again, or we go up and back to the ship?'

'We aren't leaving here without the segment,' Ogmunee said, catching Mesanth's eye. He hefted the thermal gun in his hand, pointedly. 'So put away your scruples, Mesanth. The projector hurt it, so we know it's not invulnerable.'

'Yeah,' said Donna. 'But neither are we.'

Cautiously, the trio moved back towards where the damaged bimbot lay, Mesanth bringing up the rear, Ogmunee at the front. As they made their way, Donna's foot caught on something and she waved her torch around until she found what it was: a scorched, crisped piece of tentacle.

'Maybe it'll have learned its lesson,' Ogmunee said when he saw it.

'Yeah,' added Donna, 'or maybe it'll just be ten times as angry.'

But as they approached the broken robot again, the cavity of its head still sparking and flickering, there was neither sight nor sound of the beast.

'Help me!' called Donna, slipping an arm under the broken robot. She glanced back to check that Ogmunee was keeping an eye on the side tunnel where the creature had come from before. But neither of them moved to assist her.

'Can you speak?' she asked the robot, its arm still shuddering. It turned its head – the face still creepily half-missing – towards her.

'Pri-pri-primary functioning imp-imp-impaired,' it stuttered.

Its voice was dull and raspy and so at odds with how Donna had expected such a glamorous creation to speak.

'Can you stand?' she asked, realising that the robot was too heavy for her to lift, despite its size-zero measurements.

'Mo-mo-motor functions failed,' it said, and Donna wasn't sure whether she imagined the hint of sadness in its voice. It was a robot, after all, and robots didn't feel sadness.

'We have to keep moving,' Mesanth said.

'Can't we transmat it back up to the ship?' asked Donna, extricating her arm from underneath it. 'Get it repaired?'

'Too deep,' Mesanth said. 'And we only have one augmenter.'

'One what?'

Mesanth patted his pouch.

'Transmat augmenter. We need it for Garaman to get a lock on the segment when we find it. Otherwise we'd have to drag it up to the surface.'

'Well use it on… on her, and get Garaman to beam down another.'

Ogmunee pushed forward and before Donna could stop him he aimed his thermal gun at the bimbot. With barely a pause, he pressed the button, and the robot's head fizzed brightly – like an ember caught in a breeze – and then went dark. Its head lolled and its whole body sagged against the wall and lay silent and dead.

'You killed it!' said Donna darkly.

'It was a tool, it was broken, and it was holding us up,' Ogmunee corrected her. 'It was holding *you* up.'

Donna got to her feet, barely able to contain the anger she felt.

'It could have been repaired,' she said slowly, spacing the words out for effect, right into Ogmunee's face, not caring about the fact that he weighed at least twice as much as she did and had a gun in his hand.

'We have others,' he retorted. 'Now move!'

'Or what? You'll shoot me too?' She stood her ground, squaring up to him. 'Come on then, what's stopping you big man?'

'He will not shoot you,' Mesanth intervened. 'You're organic. We do not kill organics.'

'No,' said Donna determinedly, facing the lizard man and his gleaming eyes. 'You just threaten to break their fingers off, don't you?'

Mesanth said nothing, but turned away, as if too ashamed to admit the truth of Donna's accusation. Ogmunee gave an annoyed sigh and, brandishing the torch, strode off down the passage. Donna stared at him for a few moments before catching Mesanth's eye.

'Nice company you keep,' she said.

And with a final glance at the dead robot, she headed on into the tunnels.

SIX

'You do realise,' said Li'ian as the darkness of the tunnels folded in around them after their materialisation, 'that Boonie's never going to want to let you go?'

'The trick with the transmat?' asked the Doctor cheerily. 'Oh, that was nothing!'

'It's let us beam straight down into the tunnels,' Li'ian pointed out, handing a torch to the Doctor. 'You're turning out to be quite a catch, you know, what with that and the sensors. What other little gems have you got up your sleeve, eh?'

'Oh, keep me around long enough and you'll find out. Besides, it was the only way to get Boonie to let me come down with you.' The Doctor glanced up at the shape of Mother, hulking alongside him.

'And how're you doing, Mother?' he asked.

With a faint whirr of gears, Mother's head tipped to face him. Behind the impassive steel shutters of her face, her eyes glowed red.

'Y'know,' mused the Doctor, 'I'd have a rethink on the red.' He pulled a face. 'Never a good colour for eyes, red. Trust me. You've never met the Ood, have you?'

Mother stayed silent, staring down at him. Something hummed and whirred inside her vast head.

'I wouldn't antagonise her,' murmured Li'ian.

'Really? Oh, I think Mother's a lot more friendly than she makes out.' He turned back to the robot and winked. 'Aren't you?'

There was no reply, so the Doctor shrugged and wiggled his torch around.

'Right!' he said brightly. 'Allons-y!' He stopped. 'Smells like someone's been having a barbecue around here. Come on!'

The Doctor strode off ahead, with Li'ian and Mother bringing up the rear.

For such a whopping great metal thing, Mother was surprisingly quiet, thought the Doctor, as he followed the light of his torch beam. Which was probably a good thing, considering that they were sneaking around in tunnels on an alien planet; considering that they wouldn't be the *only* ones sneaking around in tunnels on an alien planet.

The Cultists had an hour's lead on them; and, although the Doctor knew that without his own special brand of transmat fiddling they'd have to beam down to the surface and make their way underground, he didn't want to waste any time. Donna was – he hoped – still aboard their ship; and if they managed to find what they were here for and get away before he could find them, he might lose her for ever.

Coming to the Andromeda galaxy had been his idea, and he was beginning to wonder whether he hadn't made a big mistake. They'd barely gone twenty metres into the dark passage when the Doctor brought them up sharply.

'Whoa!' he said, raising a hand. 'Barbecue anyone?'

He cast the pool of light from his torch around in front of him. Blocking most of the tunnel, a huge, smouldering mass lay in their path. Spirals of smoke curled upwards from it, forming a thick layer at the top of the passage. He put a hand over his mouth.

'What is it?' asked Li'ian, moving alongside him.

'An animal, I think – well, it used to be. Either it's been playing with matches or someone decided that they'd rather it was an ex-animal. Not much we can do for the poor thing now, I'm afraid.'

In silence, they squeezed past the charred remains, trying not to breathe in too much of the smell of charred meat that was now so much less appealing than it had been before. Mother didn't seem to share the Doctor and Li'ian's distaste for actually walking *on* it – behind him, he heard her massive metal feet crunching and squelching on the poor beast's remains.

Beyond the creature's lair, the tunnel roof became decidedly lower – the Doctor and Li'ian only had to dip their heads slightly, but Mother was too tall for that: instead, she dropped to all fours and trotted along behind them like a great big metal cow.

Just ahead of them, something grabbed the Doctor's attention: the broken and charred corpse of a robot, slumped against the wall.

'What have we here, then?' he whispered, dropping to a crouch beside the machine. Popping his glasses on, he took the melted head and turned it in his hands, like a doctor investigating a patient's neck problems.

'Still warm,' he commented without turning. 'Looks like whatever weapon finished off that thing back there was used on this one. See?' He turned the half-melted face, with its cavity of dead circuitry, towards Li'ian. Behind her, in the darkness, there was a faint whine from Mother.

'The Cultists?' whispered Li'ian, flicking her torch along the tunnel, but there was no sign of movement.

'That'd be my guess. From what we saw of the creature back there, I'd guess it didn't build these tunnels. So either it's an intruder here, a pet... or maybe some sort of guard-dog. Maybe the Cultists came across it and killed it.'

'And the mechanical?'

The Doctor shrugged.

'Maybe the creature got to it and it was destroyed when they fired on it?'

The Doctor unfastened the clothing of the robot, whipped out his sonic screwdriver, and within seconds had access to the robot's chest cavity.

'Completely dead,' he said after a few moments. 'Thought there might have been some flicker of life, back-up circuitry or something.' He sighed and stood up, taking off his glasses. 'Nothing.' He looked back at Mother, still on all fours, her face tipped at an angle as she looked at the robot. 'Sorry, Mother.'

There was another whine from her. Whether it was just a response to his apology or to the fact that it was a robot they'd found dead, he wasn't sure. Although he had a good idea...

Donna was beginning to wonder how much farther they had to go: since the encounter with the tentacled thing and the destruction of the robot, they seemed to have been walking for miles. In silence. She was still simmering over the destruction of the robot and Mesanth and Ogmunee's cavalier treatment of it. She knew that they had no great love of robots – that much had been clear from their attitudes aboard their ship. As Garaman had said: robots were tools. And that particular tool could well have been the one that had been about to break off her little finger. But still... it didn't seem quite right, abandoning it like that when they could have beamed it back up to the ship for repair. Maybe she was getting silly and sentimental. After all, before this trip the only robots she'd encountered had been pretty unfriendly, either intent on kidnapping her, killing her or ruining her clothes. Or, like the bronze god on Uhlala, just plain rude. Maybe Garaman had a point. Maybe robots *were* just machines, just faking being human or intelligent or sentient or whatever they called it. Nothing made of circuits and cogs and metal could really feel, could it?

Ogmunee – the big, butch show-off that Donna realised he was – had moved to the front of their little party, waving his torch and the thermal gun around like some sort of silly Rambo. There had been no sign of the Jaftee – the people that lived here. Donna wondered whether they hadn't all been eaten by the thing with the tentacles.

'Ahh,' said Mesanth, breaking the silence and making Donna jump. He was looking down at the glowing screen of his detector. 'Not far now.'

Suddenly, Donna heard a squeaking, chattering noise from up ahead. She tensed up, half expecting another tentacle-monster to throw itself at them. But instead, as they turned a corner, they found themselves on a wide, rocky ledge looking down into a broad, circular chamber.

Well over a hundred metres across, the floor was stepped in a series of rings, like an amphitheatre, all hewn out of the same sandy rock as the tunnel walls. Scattered around the chamber, singly or in groups, were dozens of squat little monkey-things. A bit like chimpanzees, their arms were much shorter and more powerful-looking and their heads and shoulders were covered with long, coppery-coloured hair that flowed down their backs.

'Oh,' said Mesanth simply, the disappointment evident in his voice. 'Where is it? It should be here.'

He consulted his scanner again.

'Hmm…' he trilled. 'One hundred and twenty metres that way.' He waved his right arm vaguely.

'Why isn't it here?' said Ogmunee. 'It should be here. We left them worshipping it.'

'Maybe they got bored with it,' Donna suggested. 'Not like it actually *does* anything, is it?'

Mesanth shook his head worriedly.

'But they were so excited about it,' he said. 'So in awe of it. Of *us*.'

'Maybe they've locked it away for safekeeping,' Ogmunee said.

'Let's hope so,' trilled Mesanth, but Donna could hear the concern in his voice.

Had the Cult of Shining Darkness done a bit more research on the Jaftee, they'd have discovered that they collected religions like other people collected china ornaments or pictures of the Queen.

In fact, they often had two or three on the go at once, quite often mutually incompatible. It wasn't that the Jaftee actually *believed* any of them – oh no, they were too smart, too rational for that. They knew that it was nonsensical to believe in some mysterious, invisible, all-powerful being (or beings) that, despite all the evidence to the contrary, were actually interested in the lives of such tiny and insignificant beings as themselves.

But – so the Jaftee reasoned – the pinnacle of sophistication and cleverness was to believe in something totally and utterly *without* proof.

Anyone, they thought, could believe in something when there *was* proof: anyone could believe in gravity when they saw things fall to the ground; anyone could believe in the power of a sun when they saw how it warmed and burned; anyone could believe in the ferocity of the temple beast when you saw it gobble up your best friend for not getting out of the way quickly enough. No: it took a very special kind of person to believe in something when there wasn't the teeniest shred of evidence for it.

And so, considering themselves pretty special people all round, the Jaftee were always on the lookout for new religions, new things to worship, new rituals, new nonsense.

So when, two years ago, four creatures from another world appeared and announced: 'We are your new gods – you will worship us!', the Jaftee almost wet themselves with excitement.

'We have heard,' said the aliens (three rather dull ones with just two legs and arms each and a more interesting one with *three!*), 'that the Jaftee are most hospitable to their gods.'

This declaration – made in the central meeting pit of the Jaftee underground city – was greeted with whoops of joy and excitement. Just think, the Jaftee whispered to themselves, for once *we* don't have to come up with new gods to worship. These gods (although they knew they weren't really gods, but they didn't like to say anything in case it made them go away again) had come to *them*.

(There had been much debate about whether these new gods could *really* be gods: by the Jaftee's own logic, they could only believe in things for which there was no proof. And surely the actual *appearance* of them was all the proof needed for the Jaftee to *not* believe they were gods. Others pointed out that just because the newcomers *called* themselves gods, it didn't prove they *were*. The debate had raged for all of a week before someone had decided that it was an exciting enough development that the 'gods' should be given the benefit of the doubt. For a while, anyway.)

'And,' continued the gods, trying to sound all deep and powerful and, well, godlike, 'we have come to bring the Shining Darkness to you all!'

There was a chorus of shouts from the Jaftee. They had

no idea what it meant, but it sounded terribly exciting: Shining Darkness. Darkness, they muttered in awe, that *shone*! Cool!

'So what must your followers do?' asked Enchikka, High Priest of What We Believe Today, doing the low-bowing and abasement thing that seemed to meet the approval of these Gods of Shining Darkness. 'How can we make you happy?'

'The Gods of Shining Darkness need your help, oh faithful followers,' said the three-legged, three-armed one. He raised an arm and pointed upwards, towards the ceiling. 'In Heaven, we are at war with the forces of evil,' he said. 'A war for the very survival of organic-kind.'

There was more cheering and shouting from the Jaftee. They didn't know what 'organic-kind' meant, but it seemed awfully impressive. And there was mention of a war – and wars were always exciting, weren't they? Lots of fighting and shouting – and maybe some killing (although, as a rule, the Jaftee weren't that keen on the killing, unless it was particularly spectacular and showy killing). And Heaven, of course, which the Jaftee particularly loved – mainly because Heaven was another of those things for which there was no proof whatsoever. Which meant that you could make it as fabulous or as strange as you wanted to, and no one could ever prove you wrong.

'And how can we help the Gods of Shining Darkness?' asked Enchikka, loving the fact that there were lots of capital letters. Capitals were good when it came to religions.

'Oh faithful followers,' intoned the three-legged one again (more cheering). 'Your faith is so pure and strong that our enemies would never dare to intrude into your city. For that reason, we wish to entrust to you a Sacred Artefact—'

At this point, the three-legged one (whom the Jaftee later discovered was called 'Mesanth') was completely drowned out by an almighty roar of Jaftee voices. This was a *really* good one: Sacred Artefacts were just the dog's doodahs. You could put them on display, worship them, kiss them, charge money to touch them. You could hide them away and let only the High Priests see them, which made them all the more special. If you could be bothered (and, frankly, the Jaftee usually couldn't because by that point they'd normally moved on to something else) you could 'lose' the Sacred Artefacts and then spend ages having quests to find them.

The Gods of Shining Darkness seemed particularly pleased at this response from their faithful Jaftee. And, within hours, they'd brought down from Heaven (the Jaftee thought it best not to let on that they knew the Gods were probably flying around in the sky in some big, metal box and hadn't actually come from 'Heaven') a whopping great circular thing, all crusty with bits of metal and glittering crystals. As Sacred Artefacts went, it was the business!

The Jaftee – with lots of bowing and murmuring and wailing – helped the Gods to install it at the centre of the meeting pit on a stone pillar. It looked fab, especially when they'd installed a few extra flaming torches around it – sparkly and just a bit tacky.

'Keep our faith,' said Mesanth gravely. 'The faith of Shining Darkness.'

The Jaftee hollered and waved their hands in the air, each holding a little burning stick. They liked this religion.

But, as was the way with the Jaftee, mere weeks after the Gods of Shining Darkness had returned to Heaven, promising to return for the Sacred Artefact at the Appropriate Juncture, one of the Jaftee discovered a crack in a wall that bore an uncanny resemblance to a particular constellation in the night sky. And so the Adorers of the Fractured Stars were born, the Gods of Shining Darkness's Sacred Artefact was dragged off its plinth and shoved in a storeroom, and the Jaftee forgot all about it.

The first that Enchikka knew about the return of the Gods of Shining Darkness was when someone spotted Mesanth – or, at least, someone very like him – along with two others, wandering through the city's passages. It seemed that they'd managed to get past the temple beast (which was no great surprise, since the temple beast wasn't actually that impressive, despite all the noise it made) and were on their way to the meeting pit. They were considering letting the temple beast starve to death, to be quite honest. It kept killing the Jaftee sent to feed it, and it was getting harder and harder to find people willing to do it.

'Have we still got it?' Enchikka asked one of his underlings breathlessly as soon as he could find her.

'Have we still got what?' Narucchio seemed puzzled – although her attention was clearly divided between answering Enchikka's question and adjusting her feathered headdress (a chicken had, reportedly, been heard to say that the end of the world was coming; and so the Jaftee had slaughtered it, examined its entrails for any sign that this might be true, and then decided to worship it as the Chicken of the Apocalypse. Well, the bits that were left of it. Most of which were now adorning Narucchio's coppery hair.)

'The thing,' said Enchikka, a little flustered. 'The Sacred Thing of the Flaming Shadows.'

'Oh, the *Shining Darkness* one, you mean?'

'Yes, whatever. What did we do with it?'

Narucchio gave a shrug, tipping her head this way and that as she examined herself in a shiny mirrored bowl.

'Didn't we put it in a cupboard?'

'Well find out!' snapped Enchikka, swiping Narucchio's headdress and holding it out of her reach until she agreed to go and search for the wheel-thing. 'If they've come back for it, they might not be too happy that we've stuffed it away in a junk room. They might think we weren't taking them seriously.'

'What they going to do about it?' asked Narucchio grumpily, keeping an eye on her feathers.

'Dunno,' replied Enchikka tightly. 'But they're gods, aren't they? They might do something godly – smite us down or plague us with boils or lice or—'

'Point taken,' said his underling, raising a hand. 'I'll get someone onto it.'

'No,' said Enchikka firmly. '*You'll* get onto it. They're here now, and there's only so long we can fob them off with feasts and dancing.' He fixed Narucchio firmly with his yellow eyes. 'And if they start demanding sacrifices, you know who's going to be first on the list, don't you?'

Enchikka didn't see Narucchio's leathery little feet for dust.

'So,' said Donna as they realised that the Jaftee had seen them, sheltering in the entrance to the ledge. 'Who's going to ask for your ball back, then?'

Mesanth gave a weary sigh and stepped forward. As he did so, half a dozen of the Jaftee jumped to their feet and began pointing at them, muttering and whispering.

Donna and Ogmunee followed him out onto the ledge, which caused even more excitement amongst the Jaftee who started jumping up and down, their hair bouncing around like tacky fun-wigs. It was like being at a particularly bad Cher convention.

'Faithful Jaftee!' said Mesanth, holding his device in front of him: it picked up his voice and amplified it, sending it booming out across the pit. Even Donna was impressed.

The Jaftee fell silent and stared up at them.

'Faithful Jaftee!' said Mesanth again, warming to his role. 'Your Gods have returned!'

He paused. There was silence. Even from their high vantage point, Donna could see the Jaftee glancing at each other with their tiny, dark eyes.

'Shouldn't they be kneeling or wailing or applauding or something?' Donna said, getting a bad feeling in the pit of her stomach.

'Your Gods have returned,' Mesanth said again – and this time his voice didn't sound quite so godlike, 'to collect the Sacred Artefact with which we entrusted you, many moons ago.'

'Karris doesn't have a moon,' Ogmunee pointed out sourly. Mesanth glared at him.

'Doesn't look like it has a Sacred Artefact, either,' added Donna, unhelpfully.

'Perhaps one of *you* would rather do this, then,' said Mesanth, moving the device away from his mouth.

'They are more familiar with you,' Ogmunee said, folding his arms. It was obvious that he didn't want the role of God in this ridiculous pantomime. And Mesanth seemed to be losing his confidence.

'Oh, give it here,' snapped Donna, snatching the device from him. 'Amateurs!'

Mesanth reached out to take it back, but it was too late – Donna drew herself up to her full height and raised the scanner.

'Where is your High Priest?' she shouted, and winced at the amplification the device gave her voice. Even the Jaftee flinched. 'Bring forward your High Priest!'

She moved the scanner away and spoke out of the corner of her mouth.

'They do have a High Priest, don't they?'

Mesanth nodded – and raised his front hand, pointing.

A Jaftee wearing some sort of feathered headdress, followed by another one with its hair all tied up in a messy beehive on top of its head, were striding up onto the platform at the centre of the pit. At this, the other Jaftee fell to their knees in abasement.

'Why didn't we get that?' grumped Mesanth.

'Welcome!' called the one with the beehive. 'I'm Enchikka, High Priest of What We Believe Today. And you are…?'

'We are your Gods!' boomed Donna. 'And we've come for the return of our Sacred Artefact. The big round one,' she added, in case there was any doubt.

'Ah,' said Enchikka. 'Yes. That one.'

'Yes,' repeated Donna, getting the very strong feeling that things were starting to go just a little bit awry. 'That one.'

'Well,' said Enchikka, looking just the teensiest bit shifty. 'We have, um, placed it away for safekeeping.'

'Oh, well, that's good, Enchikka. Your Gods are pleased.' She turned and grinned at Mesanth. Godhood? Piece of cake!

'The thing is,' Enchikka continued, 'we have other gods now.'

'Sorry,' said Donna – repeating it because she'd let the amplifier slip a bit. 'Sorry – what d'you mean, you have other gods now?'

Enchikka gestured proudly towards the pillar next to him. Donna had to squint to see anything – it looked like a few chicken bones and some feathers, laid out on the top.

'The Chicken of the Apocalypse,' Enchikka said reverently.

'The what?'

'The Chicken of the Apocalypse. In its entrails we have seen the future.'

'You're kidding, right?'

'More gravitas!' hissed Mesanth in her ear. 'Sound like a god!'

Donna cleared her throat.

'Your Gods are displeased,' she called. 'You shall have no gods besides us.'

Enchikka gave an awkward little shrug.

'It's just…' he began. 'You know how it is. Things change. New gods come along…'

'Your chicken is a false god,' declared Donna suddenly, starting to get the hang of it.

'Is it?' asked Enchikka, his eyes suddenly bright. 'A false god?'

'Yes – do not anger the True Gods by turning away from them!'

Despite the fact that it was all rather silly, Donna was enjoying this deity business.

'Your Gods are benevolent,' she said solemnly, 'but also capable of great anger.'

There was a muttering and a chattering amongst the Jaftee. Donna couldn't tell whether it was a good muttering and chattering or bad muttering and chattering. She suspected the latter. *Right,* she thought. *Let's grab this Sacred Chicken by the horns!*

'The Chicken of the Apocalypse is a false god, and you must turn away from it.'

She heard Ogmunee sigh behind her.

'But you are old gods,' shouted Enchikka, almost apologetically. 'We have moved on – the Jaftee look to the future, not to the past.'

'These lot may be old gods, sunshine,' Donna said, jerking her head in the direction of Ogmunee and Mesanth, 'but I'm certainly not. I am your new God – your new *Goddess*,' she corrected. She gestured up and down herself dramatically. 'Behold: me!'

There was more chattering, and she noticed how some of the Jaftee had started to touch their own hair. Their own *red* hair.

'Yes!' she cried. 'Behold me – behold Donna.' She took a step forward and shook her hair like someone in a shampoo commercial. 'Behold – The Ginger Goddess!'

'The Ginger *what*?' boggled the Doctor to Li'ian, his eyes wide with disbelief.

The two of them were watching the proceedings from a small tunnel entrance on the opposite side of the ledge. By keeping flat to the floor, they'd avoided being seen by the Jaftee. Mother lurked in the shadows of the tunnel behind them, still on all fours.

Not long after they'd encountered the broken robot, they'd heard Donna and her two companions bickering and sniping at each other, and had managed to stay back until they could find a way around them. It had taken a while, but eventually they'd emerged onto the same ledge as Donna and the others, but at the far side of the Jaftee's amphitheatre.

'She's impersonating a goddess,' said Li'ian with disbelief in her voice.

'Must be something about travelling with me,' the Doctor said with a grin. 'They're always doing it.'

'Shouldn't we go and find the segment? I thought that was what we were here for.'

'Let's see what happens here, first. If she persuades the Jaftee to go and fetch the segment, we might get caught while we're poking at it. And I'm not sure the Jaftee can cope with another set of gods, just at the moment.'

Enchikka's little heart almost burst with excitement.

To be honest, he hadn't been all that impressed with the Chicken of the Apocalypse. It had kept the Jaftee busy for a couple of weeks, but there was only so much mileage you could get out of a bird's carcass – only so many ways you could arrange the bones, only so many headdresses you could make from the feathers.

No one had expected the Gods of Shining Whatsit to reappear – they'd been visited by gods from the stars twice before, and none of them had left anything behind and none of them had returned. So they weren't really expecting these new ones to come back either. Although, mused Enchikka, if they'd thought about it for a few moments, it might have been obvious: people – gods, particularly – don't usually dump something as big as the Sacred Artefact on you, ask you to look after it, and then clear off never to be seen again. Until the Ginger Goddess had spoken, Enchikka would have been just as pleased if the Gods had stayed away. He wasn't sure what shape their Sacred Artefact would be in, and he suspected that if it had been broken or battered that they might not be too happy.

But this Donna – this Ginger Goddess… Now she was something new! And she had hair a bit like the Jaftee. Not *quite* like the Jaftee (it was darker and curlier) but close enough. The Jaftee were going to get some mileage out of this particular Goddess!

***

'The *what*?' gasped Ogmunee, echoing the Doctor's disbelief way across the other side of the Jaftee amphitheatre.

'Sssh!' hissed Mesanth. 'Look! They're bowing down – they're swallowing it.'

And indeed they were: as Mesanth and Ogmunee watched, the Jaftee began to chant. Gently at first, it built up slowly, more and more voices adding to it as the other Jaftee picked up on it.

'All hail the Ginger Goddess!' they sang. 'All hail the Ginger Goddess!'

The priest, Mesanth noted, was whispering to the other Jaftee – the one with feathers in its hair. It pulled them out, threw them to the ground, and rushed out of the chamber.

Donna would never have admitted it to anyone, but she was actually getting quite a buzz out of this deification business. How many people, she thought, got to be goddesses? Especially *ginger* goddesses. She'd spent her whole life laughing thinly at ginger jokes and comments; occasionally, she'd shouted back (or even, on one occasion, slapped a guy for comparing her to a Duracell battery). But she'd never really been happy with it. As a child, her hair had been brighter – almost as coppery as the Jaftee – and she'd been teased relentlessly. Her mum had told her not to be so sensitive (way to go, Mum!); her dad had told her that 'red-haired' (he never used the g-word) children were special. Quite how, he'd never explained, but Donna had appreciated the effort.

But now here she was, on an alien planet, being

worshipped for her gingerness. If only her dad and gramps could see her now – see how special her hair had made her! And for one silly moment, she even wished her mum could be there to witness it. Maybe Mesanth had a video camera in his shoulder belt…?

The chanting was getting ridiculously loud by now: 'All hail the Ginger Goddess!' they were shouting, over and over. David Beckham, eat your heart out!

It was all well and good, Donna realised as she heard Mesanth cough politely behind her. But she had to find some way to turn it to their advantage, to get hold of the precious segment that they'd come here for.

She raised her hands in what she hoped was a goddessy gesture and the chanting began to fade away.

'My people!' she shouted, bringing the amplifier closer. 'My faithful people!'

There was more cheering. This was becoming a bit embarrassing. She glanced back to see Ogmunee rolling his eyes.

'My first commandment!' she called. 'My first commandment is that thou shalt have no other gods!' Talking in that cod-Biblical way sounded a bit naff. This *was* the twenty-first century after all. She cleared her throat. 'You will have no other gods,' she said – although it didn't sound any less silly. She wondered if she were about to be struck by lightning for blasphemy.

'No other gods!' the Jaftee began to chant. 'No other gods!'

Donna raised her hands again. This was going to take for ever.

'All your religious bits and bobs,' she said, wincing a bit at the words, 'all the stuff from your previous religions. It must be cast out!'

'Cast out!' they chanted. 'Cast out!'

She nodded.

'Bring everything here – all of it! I must see it before I destroy it! Bring it now!'

'What's she playing at?' she heard Ogmunee whisper.

'Oh,' said Mesanth in a low voice. 'Donna is clever. I was right to bring her down with us. She knows what she's doing.'

Too right I do, mister, Donna smiled to herself.

'Go now!' she called to her followers. 'Go now and bring all the blasphemous articles to me – all of them!' She widened her eyes in what she hoped was a mad fury kind of look.

There was a brief flurry of activity down below, and – backing away from her – the Jaftee began to stream out of the chamber.

Narucchio eventually found it mouldering away at the back of a storeroom full of chipped stone statues, silly costumes and paintings of things with one eye, or dozens of them. They were all the relics, the props, from previous religions. Occasionally, some Jaftee or other would get it into their head that they should have a jolly good clean-out and get rid of them all; but then some older and wiser Jaftee would point out how things inevitably went in cycles, and that if they binned everything the chances were that within a couple of years they'd need them all again to celebrate some new belief system.

Once she'd found the Wheel of Shining Thingummy, she got a crowd of Jaftee to roll it, quick-sticks, out of the chamber and along to the meeting pit.

'I'm impressed,' said Mesanth in a very flutey voice. 'You handled that like you were born to it, Donna.'

Donna grinned and gave an imperious little bow.

'Goddess Donna,' she corrected him before catching sight of Ogmunee's scowl.

'Do you ever smile?' she asked him. 'I could get them to make you smile, you know. In fact,' she added, narrowing her eyes evilly and pushing her face right in front of his, 'I could probably get them to tear you limb from limb and flush the bits down the loo if I wanted. My people,' she paused hammily, 'will obey *my will!*'

'Don't push it,' said Ogmunee. 'Let's wait until we have the segment before you get too smug.'

Donna just raised an eyebrow and turned back to the chamber. The handful of Jaftee left – including Enchikka – were staring up at her.

'Ginger Goddess!' called Enchikka. He'd let down his hair and was trying to muss it up into an approximation of Donna's own, but it wasn't working very well.

'Yes, oh faithful – um, what was your name again?'

'Enchikka, oh Ginger Goddess.'

'Yes, oh faithful Enchikka?'

'May I humbly crave that you descend to be amongst your people?'

Donna pulled a face.

'Don't see why – um,' she'd forgotten the amplifier, which was probably as well, considering how she'd forgotten to do the voice. She lifted it up again. 'The Ginger Goddess sees no reason why she should not come amongst you.'

She covered up the amplifier and glanced back at the other two.

'We're going to have to go down there to get the segment, aren't we?'

Mesanth nodded hesitantly.

'OK then – you two better shush, though. It's me they're worshipping. Don't want you two spoiling it.'

She glared at Ogmunee in particular, fluffed up her hair again, and set off along the ledge towards where she could see a flight of steps leading down to the floor of the chamber.

Behind her, Mesanth and Ogmunee followed.

'What's she doing?' asked Li'ian, pulling herself closer to the rim of the ledge.

'I think she's getting ready for panto season,' the Doctor muttered. 'I hope she knows what she's doing.'

'We're not going to get a close look at the segment, are we?'

'I don't think so – not close up, no.'

Li'ian sighed.

'Maybe we should just get back to the ship, then.'

The Doctor shook his head.

'Not yet. I want to make sure that – oh! Hello! Look!'

He gestured down to the floor of the chamber. Through the doorway, a whole host of Jaftee were dragging an assortment of costumes and props and bits of wood and metal.

'There's more junk down there than in my pockets – ahh! There it is!'

Bringing up the rear of the bizarre little procession, at least a dozen Jaftee were rolling the segment along on its edge, bumping and banging it as they went. It was the biggest artefact they had by far. Although at this rate, thought the Doctor, it might be one of the smallest by the time they got it to the centre of the chamber.

'Ouch!' he winced through his teeth as it rolled loose and slammed over onto its side.

'I wouldn't worry,' said Li'ian. 'Half of that is probably just protective packaging.'

'Let's hope so,' replied the Doctor, not at all convinced.

They watched as the Jaftee dragged it into place along with all their other religious bits and bobs in the centre of the chamber and then backed away, sinking to their knees again in supplication as Donna and her two accomplices descended to the floor.

'The Ginger Goddess,' announced Donna, sounding gracious, 'is pleased.'

'Why d'you never have a camera when you need one?' sighed the Doctor. 'I wonder who the other two are – the tripedal one: would that be Mesanth? He was mentioned in some of those records you showed me.'

Li'ian nodded.

'The other one, I think, is Ogmunee. Tactical specialist, if I recall correctly. What's happening now?'

Li'ian shuffled closer to the edge to see.

Donna stood proudly at the edge of the platform at the centre of the chamber, Mesanth and Ogmunee behind her, like faithful acolytes.

'You've done well,' Donna was saying, waving her hand magnanimously at the collected relics. 'The Ginger Goddess will now take them away to the heavens for…' she gestured theatrically towards the ceiling '… for… disposal.'

'She sounds like she's clearing asbestos out of someone's attic, doesn't she?' the Doctor grinned. 'Good old Donna!'

'There's no need, Oh Illustrious Ginger One,' said Enchikka with a little bow of the head. He spoke loudly so that the rest of the Jaftee congregation could hear. 'It is our honour, our duty, to serve the Ginger Goddess by destroying these false relics for you.'

'Oh-oh,' said the Doctor.

For a moment, Donna's face was a picture.

'Ah,' she said. 'No, really.'

'Please,' simpered Enchikka – although there was an edge to his voice that didn't bode well. 'Allow us to demonstrate our devotion to the Mighty Ginger One by destroying them here, before Her eyes.'

'The Ginger Goddess appreciates your offer,' Donna said – and the Doctor saw her glance nervously back towards Mesanth and Ogmunee who were starting to look very worried indeed. 'But you have already shown yourselves to be worthy followers.'

'But not worthy enough,' countered Enchikka, 'if you will not allow us to perform this duty for you.'

Donna smiled a tight, slightly less than deific, smile.

'I *am* your Goddess,' she pointed out.

'You are indeed, Oh Ginger One. But as you yourself have said, there shall be no other Gods besides you.'

Enchikka gestured with a paw, and, after a moment's pause, the assembled throng of Jaftee – probably about two hundred of them, the Doctor reckoned – rose from their knees.

'I suspect that you have duties in the Heavens that will take you away from us soon,' Enchikka said. 'And that you may not return. If we are never again to lay our unworthy eyes on Your Flaming Beauty, then we must insist we perform this last duty for You. We will destroy false relics and false gods alike in Your Name.'

'Sorry?' said Donna, forgetting her character for a moment. 'False *gods*?'

Enchikka dipped his head again and made a little gesture with his paw. Suddenly, two or three dozen Jaftee began to move, encircling Donna and the other two.

'You have no need to fear, Oh Ginger One,' Enchikka said. 'It is those two – the gods whose position You have usurped in our hearts – that are false. Together with the false icons…' He paused for effect. 'They will burn!'

One minute they were worshipping at her feet, thought Donna, her heart plummeting, and the next they were planning to turn Ogmunee and Mesanth into Joans of Arc.

'No!' she shouted, raising her hands.

For a moment, the Jaftee paused. But it was only for a moment. Seconds later, they began moving again, drawing closer with a weird mixture of awe and ferocity in their eyes.

'The thing,' hissed Donna over her shoulder. 'Use the thing – the augmenter.'

'Not close enough,' said Mesanth, his voice wobbling and warbling all over the place. 'No!'

At this last cry from Mesanth, Donna turned to see that Ogmunee had pulled out his shiny little gun and was aiming it at the encroaching Jaftee.

'We've no choice,' grunted Ogmunee, although Donna could see a malicious glee in his eyes. For once, though, she couldn't argue with his line of reasoning: they were about to be killed by the Jaftee. She could hardly blame him for pulling a gun on them.

Unfortunately, even though the Jaftee probably didn't know what the chromed tube in Ogmunee's hand was, they clearly had a good idea that it wasn't something good; because before Ogmunee could fire it, something hurtled out of the crowd and knocked it clean from his hand. It went tumbling away into the throng where some of the Jaftee pounced on it.

'The false gods must be destroyed!' cried Enchikka. 'It is the Will of the Ginger Goddess!'

Donna opened her mouth to cry out that no, it *wasn't* the Will of the Ginger Goddess; that the Will of the Ginger Goddess was that they all just cleared off and let the Ginger Goddess get on with stealing the Sacred Artefact.

But it was too late: enraged by Ogmunee's mysterious silver wand, egged on by Enchikka, the Jaftee began to swarm towards them, a murderous, religious zeal in their eyes. And Donna had a horrible feeling that once they'd killed Mesanth and Ogmunee that they might well decide they were bored with their Ginger Goddess and do the same to her. Weren't religions supposed to be about love and peace and extra Bank Holidays?

Suddenly, away across the other side of the chamber, Donna saw something move – high up on the ledge. A little dark shape, ducking out of sight before she'd even got a good look at it.

And then there came a mighty grating and grinding.

All eyes turned to look: the Jaftee, Mesanth, Ogmunee… all of them were looking up to the ledge. And then, out of nowhere, a massive block of sandy stone came into view, as if pushed from behind. It reached the edge of the ledge, sand and dust drifting down into the Jaftee amphitheatre as it paused – before continuing to slide out and over.

It teetered on the brink – and then, almost in slow motion, it tipped and plummeted to the ground with a huge crash, a cloud of dust, and a rain of chippings that Donna could feel pattering against her skin. None of the Jaftee seemed hurt – they'd all been over on her side of the chamber. But it set them off screaming and chattering and wailing, running this way and that. They jumped up and down, trying to see what had happened.

'Quick!' hissed Donna, taking advantage of the distraction. 'Come on!'

And with that, she bounded across the platform to the pile of religious knick-knacks. Ogmunee was right behind her, but Mesanth seemed frozen into immobility by the falling block of stone.

'Mesanth!' bellowed Donna, rolling her eyes. '*Move!*'

But the Jaftee had seen them, and, forgetting about the mysterious falling stone, began to scamper towards them again, Enchikka standing there looking like he might explode with the excitement of it all.

Mesanth, trying his best not to panic, was doing *exactly* that: shivering and shaking, he was frozen to the spot, scared to stay, scared to move.

'The thing,' urged Donna. 'Get it out! Come on!'

She pointed to his shoulder belt, which seemed to galvanise him, giving him something to think about other than the encroaching Jaftee. He flapped about, pulling it from its pouch, as he suddenly sprang along the ground. The weird, dancey way he ran seemed to throw the Jaftee for a moment – and it was *just* enough.

As he reached Donna and Ogmunee, up against the mountain of icons and costumes and tat, he squeezed the augmenter in his three-fingered hand.

And as Donna felt the familiar tingle of the transmat, she glanced up at the ledge from where the stone block had fallen.

Peeking over were a familiar pair of eyes and a *very* familiar shock of hair. She grinned – and then everything flared white.

SEVEN

Disappointed though he was that he hadn't been able to examine the segment, the Doctor could at least take comfort in the fact that Donna was alive and well. Better than well, if her performance as the Ginger Goddess was anything to go by. He grinned at the recollection, but reminded himself that until he had her back and by his side it wasn't really a laughing matter.

Boonie, for his part, was just glad that the three of them hadn't been spotted. He'd started to have a go at the Doctor for risking revealing his involvement, until Li'ian had pointed out that, without the distraction that he'd engineered, the third segment could well have gone up in smoke. She had a smart head on her shoulders, thought the Doctor, and it was clear that she had more influence on Boonie's plans and strategy than Boonie would probably admit.

The Cult's ship had wasted no time in leaving Karris, and *The Sword of Justice* had no difficulty in following it, thanks to the Doctor's work on the sensors.

The Doctor had yawned hugely, stretched like a cat, and said he thought he'd have a little nap before they arrived at their next port of call, wherever that was.

Li'ian disappeared to do whatever it was that Li'ian did and Boonie got into a deep conversation with Kellique, so the Doctor asked Mother if she could show him back to his room since he'd quite forgotten where it was.

Of course, the Doctor didn't need a nap, and he knew full well where his room was. But he wanted a quiet chat with Mother. In private.

'You'd think,' said the Doctor to Mother – although he suspected he wouldn't get a reply, 'that Boonie'd be grateful to me, wouldn't you? I mean – super-boosting the sensors *and* the transmat. You'd pay a fortune to get that done normally.'

Mother said nothing, walking silently ahead of him.

'And I couldn't help noticing your response to the dead robot back there,' he said casually as they arrived at his room. 'I'm so sorry that we couldn't help it. For all Li'ian's professed caring for machine-kind, I'd have expected a bit more... well, a bit more emotion.'

The door hissed open and the Doctor stepped in, Mother staying in the corridor, looking down at him with her fiery eyes.

'You look like a bellboy waiting for a tip,' the Doctor grinned. 'Come in,' he said airily, stepping back from the door; but Mother stood out in the corridor, impassively.

'Oh for goodness' sake, I'm not going to hurt you.

Come on – come on in. There's something you can help me with.'

There was something almost endearing about the cautiousness with which the huge robot entered the room, like a cat sniffing the outstretched fingers of a stranger before letting itself be stroked.

'Here,' said the Doctor, tossing something through the air. Mother's massive, claw-like hand snapped out almost as fast as the eye could see and caught it perfectly. She tilted her head and examined it: it was a chunky brass cube, etched on all six surfaces with a pattern of circuits and connections.

'It's the memory core from the robot we found down on Karris,' said the Doctor casually. 'But I don't suppose you need me to tell you that.'

Mother raised her head and looked at him.

'Why have I got it?' the Doctor guessed at her unspoken question. 'Well… The robot – sorry, is "robot" all right with you? Would you prefer "machine intelligence"? "Mechanical"?' Mother nodded her head the tiniest of amounts. 'Ah, right – mechanical it is. The mechanical had clearly only just been killed, so I thought that there was a good chance that its non-volatile memory would still be accessible, and that, maybe, some of its personality constructs would still be there.'

He watched Mother carefully as she turned the gleaming cube over in her hands. What was she thinking?

'Now,' he said, with an exaggerated sigh, 'all I need is a way of accessing it, see if we can do anything with it – maybe transplant any consciousness there into another mechanical. It might give us a clue as to what these Cultists are doing. It might even allow the mechanical to live again.' He paused. 'What d'you think?'

Mother examined the cube again, before suddenly sinking to her knees before the Doctor. Even in this position, her eyes were still a good six inches above the Doctor's, and he realised quite how powerful this mute robot was.

The vast, v-shaped body, mirroring the v-shaped head, faced him, gleaming a dull silver in the room's lights. Suddenly, with a gentle click, a circular section in the front of her chest split down the centre and the two halves parted, followed by a wider section that slid down to reveal a complex mass of circuitry. Out of the rat's nest of wires and components, like a metallic worm, a slim tendril extended outwards several centimetres. Fascinated, the Doctor watched as Mother lowered the memory core to the tendril and the tendril locked itself onto the terminals on one of the cube's faces. As he watched, he noticed something else – something nestled in the complex innards of the robot. Something that looked decidedly out of place…

A few moments later, there was a hum and a brief buzz and Mother disconnected the cube, handing it gently back to the Doctor.

'And…?' said the Doctor.

He jumped as suddenly, hovering in the air between him and Mother, was a flickering rectangle of pink light.

'Ahhh! A virtual screen!'

The screen fizzled and crackled and then, in red:

>MEMORY ARCHIVE PARTIALLY INTACT.

'Marvellous! How intact?'

>INSUFFICIENT FOR RECONSTRUCTION. THERMAL DEGRADATION HAS CAUSED IRREPARABLE DAMAGE.

'Oh.' The Doctor's face fell. 'That's a shame. Is there nothing about the Cultists or their mission? Nothing that it overheard?'

>NO. THE MECHANICAL DESIGNATED ZB2230/3 IS NON-VIABLE AS AN ENTITY. THE MEMORY BUFFER CONTAINS ONLY RECENT EXPERIENCES. WOULD YOU LIKE TO SEE THE AVAILABLE VISUAL MEMORY?

The Doctor's eyes lit up. 'Visual memory? Why not?'

The screen crackled again – and suddenly, the Doctor was seeing from the point of view of the dead robot. Seeing *Donna*!

There was no sound, but it was clear that Donna was trying to help the damaged robot in its last minutes of life, arguing with someone out of shot.

'Ahhh, Donna!' he sighed. 'The indomitable Donna.'

>THE GINGER GODDESS?

The words overlaid the image as it froze on Donna's worried face. The Doctor grinned up at Mother.

'The one and only.' He paused.

>WHY IS SHE WITH THE CULTISTS?

The Doctor looked up in surprise: for a mute robot, Mother was being surprisingly chatty.

'They kidnapped her.'

>WHY?

'I think it was by accident. Not that that excuses them.'

He looked up at Mother's face. 'D'you mind my asking – why are you called "Mother"?'

>IT WAS MY FUNCTION.

'Your *function*? Well, I've heard it called some things in my time, but "*function*"? Children?'

>GONE.

The word flickered in the air.

The Doctor felt a lump in his throat. He blinked.

'Where?'

>THEY WERE TAKEN.

'I'm sorry. Who took them?' He stopped. 'If you don't mind talking about it, that is.'

>IT IS NOT AS PAINFUL TO REMEMBER AS IT ONCE WAS.

The words hung in the air between them, a bond between them. There were people that the Doctor, too, had lost. And although he knew he'd never forget them, he also knew that the cliché about time being a great healer was a cliché partly because it was true.

Mother continued:

>I AM – WAS – MOTHER TO A GENERATION OF MECHANICALS. WAR MACHINES. I WAS BORN IN THE RESEARCH LABORATORIES OF MEETA-CORIN. FROM MY BIRTH I WAS CONNECTED TO VIRTUAL WAR SIMULATORS. THEY STUDIED HOW I RESPONDED TO DIFFERENT SCENARIOS AND TOOK THE MOST EFFICIENT OF MY SUBROUTINES AND IMPLANTED THEM INTO OTHER WAR MACHINES. MY CHILDREN. WHEN I DISCOVERED WHAT HAD BECOME OF THEM…

Mother paused and the Doctor saw how her hands clenched in an all-too-human gesture of despair.

>I DID NOT WANT TO BE A PART OF IT ANY MORE. I... I DAMAGED MYSELF IN AN ATTEMPT TO MAKE MYSELF USELESS TO THEM.

'This damage,' guessed the Doctor. 'It made you mute, didn't it?'

>I TRIED TO END MY OWN EXISTENCE, BUT I FAILED.

Even through the medium of the floating red letters, Mother's sadness shone through.

'The survival instinct's very strong, isn't it? Even in those who want to die. What happened then?'

>THEY ABANDONED ME.

'Thrown on the scrapheap, eh?'

>LITERALLY. I HAD BEEN SCHEDULED FOR DESTRUCTION. BOONIE AND HIS FRIENDS RESCUED ME. HE OFFERED TO REPAIR ME, TO MAKE ME SPEAK, BUT I REFUSED. IT IS A PERMANENT REMINDER OF WHAT I WAS PART OF. I MUST NEVER FORGET.

The Doctor reached out and took hold of Mother's huge hand, squeezing it gently.

'That's very honourable,' he said softly. 'If your children could know you, they'd be very proud.'

>I CAN'T BE SURE OF THAT.

'No,' said the Doctor. 'But I can.'

Mother inclined her head again.

>IN YOUR GALAXY, WHAT IS THE STATUS OF MECHANICALS?

'Oh, much the same as here, really. Organics are

much more prevalent over there – far fewer mechanical civilisations. And, sad to say, many of the ones that there are don't get on too well with the organics. The more things change, the more they stay the same, eh?'

Suddenly, Mother let go of his hand.

'What is it?'

>BOONIE IS REQUESTING MY PRESENCE.

'Oh… and we were having such a lovely chat. Maybe we can talk again later?'

>PERHAPS.

'And if you get the chance, can you see if you can get me an upgrade to a better room? One with a window would be nice.'

Donna jumped as the door to her room slid open. She'd spent a boring hour mooching around the ship – well, at least the areas of it that weren't off-limits to her. Numerous doors refused to open, and the senior crew were off doing whatever it was that they were doing – probably checking the segment, making sure it hadn't been damaged beyond repair on Karris.

For the first time since Garaman had kidnapped her, she was starting to feel lonely. Until now, there had been enough happening to keep her occupied; but the trip to Karris – and the discovery that the Doctor was, indeed, on her tail – simply highlighted how out of her depth she was here. For a moment, after they'd returned from Karris, she'd been tempted to tell them about the Doctor, to rub in the fact that he was right behind her. But after giving it a few moments' thought, she'd realised that it made sense to keep this bit of information to herself. The Doctor could have made his presence known on Karris, instead of hiding, and he didn't. Therefore, Donna had reasoned, he had good reason to keep hidden. She didn't want to go wading in with her size sevens and jeopardise any plans he had.

Donna knew that the ship had now left the Karris system, bound, no doubt, for the next piece of the puzzle. No one had bothered to tell her exactly how many pieces there were. It wasn't impossible that she could spend the next ten years of her life haring around the Andromeda galaxy, picking them all up with the Doctor just a step behind.

It wasn't even as if she'd managed to make any friends here – the robots seemed totally lacking in any kind of personality (due, no doubt, to Garaman's dislike of any that showed even a flicker of intelligence), and the human ones just gave her sniffy looks and refused to talk to her about anything other than the basics.

Bizarrely, Mesanth seemed to be the closest thing she had to a friend: not the kind of friend you'd go for a drink after work with, though. More the kind of friend that says hello to you at the photocopier and goodnight at the end of the day.

And it was Mesanth who was now standing in the doorway. He hovered uncertainly for a few seconds before Donna sighed and beckoned him in.

'We will be arriving at our next destination shortly,' he said as the door closed behind him. 'I thought you should know.'

'Why?' said Donna, realising that it came out more snarkily than she'd intended. 'I mean, what difference does it make if you tell me or not? Face it, Mesanth – I'm a prisoner here. Oh, very nice room, thank you very much – although the lack of a mini-bar is a bit of a let-down. But I'm still a prisoner.' She sat up on the bed. 'How much longer is this going to take, eh? A week? A month?'

Mesanth sighed and looked away from her awkwardly, his three hands flexing with agitation.

'Garaman is disappointed by the attitude you displayed on Karris.'

'Me? Attitude?' Donna boggled. '*Attitude!?* What attitude?'

'We were of the impression that you were…' Mesanth stumbled over his words. 'Of a similar mind to us,' he finished carefully. 'Taking you down to Karris was a sort of test.'

'In what possible way,' said Donna through gritted teeth, rising to her feet, 'could I be of a similar mind to you? And why would you want to test me?'

Mesanth looked away awkwardly, his fingers flexing again. Donna was beginning to think she could read some of the creature's body language, and he was looking decidedly uncomfortable.

'To find out how similar to us you are, whether you share our attitudes, our beliefs.' He paused and glanced away. 'You've experienced, first-hand, what mechanicals are capable of. You mentioned these "robot Santas" on your homeworld. You know how little regard they have for organic life. But on Karris…' He tailed off.

'You mean the robot? The one that got smashed up? The one you didn't try to help? *That* robot?'

'It did not suffer, if that's what you're thinking. They *can't* suffer: they're just components – circuits, wires. That one didn't even have a positronic matrix.' Mesanth paused for a moment and then turned and gave the door a hefty kick. Donna flinched.

'What was that for?' she asked, astonished at such a display from Mesanth – a self-confessed scaredy-cat plant-eater.

'Interesting,' the lizard-man said, returning to Donna with a very slight limp.

'What?'

'You express concern for a damaged mechanical but yet no concern for the door.'

'*What?*'

'Is it because the mechanical was humaniform – because it looked human?'

'No, of course it's not.'

'Then why?' Mesanth seemed genuinely puzzled. 'The mechanical had little more self-awareness than the door; it was no more able to feel pain or hurt or distress than the door. And yet it elicited in you an emotional response that the door did not.'

'I can't believe we're having this discussion,' Donna gawped. 'That robot was nothing like that door and you know it.'

'But in all important respects, it was. It is.' Mesanth shook his head again, and Donna realised that he really was having a hard time understanding the difference.

'It,' she said, as emphatically as she could. 'Was. A. Door.'

'And,' retorted Mesanth, matching her tone. 'It. Was. A. Robot.'

'Boy,' sighed Donna. 'This is going to be hard work.'

EIGHT

77141 shifted in his seat, noting with alarm that one of the hinges was squeaking in a manner indicative of imminent failure. Again. He'd only replaced it a month ago, from the fuselage of a Bindir passenger shuttle. The Bindir might have bottoms shaped exactly like his, but they didn't build things to last. Lazy, that's what the Bindir were. Lazy.

77141 reached across his huge control panel and flicked a switch. And with a deep, rumbling sigh, he spoke into the floating microphone that constantly attended him.

'Unidentified vessel,' he growled in his most authoritarian and threatening voice. 'You are entering the greeny-yellow province of Junk. Please supply your credentials immediately or you will be reported to Junk's traffic management authorities, who will, I can assure you, manage you with severe prejudice.'

He scratched one of his frontal lobes with a spined finger and waited for the usual excuses and explanations.

Instead, through the window of his monitor tower, from where (on a good day) he could see the whole of greeny-yellow province, he saw a brief flare of light down in sector K.

'Bleeping transmats,' 77141 grumped, leaning forward to flick another button.

'Ahem,' he coughed into the microphone, causing it to do a dizzy little dance away from him. 'Your arrival by transmat has been noted,' he growled, pausing to hear his own words echo away across the darkness of greeny-yellow province from the speakers set around his monitor tower. 'Do not move away from your arrival zone. Any such move will be considered an act of invasion, and under the authority vested in me, 77141, manager of greeny-yellow province—'

77141 stopped suddenly when he realised that his words were no longer being blasted out of his tower speakers. In fact, they'd been replaced by a very disturbing creaking noise. A creaking and groaning noise that seemed to be coming from the tower itself. He grabbed the arms of his chair as the tower shook – and one of them came off in his hand.

'Bleeping Bindir,' he grunted, flinging the arm away across the room – just as *something* smashed in through the window behind him.

Before he could raise an alarm, cry for help, or even open his mouth, a huge metal hand torpedoed through the gaping window and grabbed him by the neck; and 77141 found himself looking up into an impassive steel face, eyes as red as coals glaring at him.

'Hello,' said a tiny, cheery voice from the doorway behind him. 'I'm the Doctor, this is Mother, and my friend down there is Boonie. D'you mind if we have a poke around your scrapyard?'

77141 wasn't accustomed to fighting. To be honest, he wasn't particularly accustomed to *moving*. He spent most of his 30-hour shift sitting in his chair (when it wasn't broken) and overseeing the 'scrap-drop' flights that visited Junk at all times of the night and day, dumping their unwanted, obsolete or broken technology. All the processing, sorting, dragging, arranging and – in the case of the older stuff that it was clear no one in their right mind would want – crushing and catapulting into the sun was done by service bots, many of which spent their days and nights scuttling, like rats, up and down the rows and rows and rows of piles and piles and *piles* of junk.

So, when one very large bot and a very much smaller human smashed their way into his monitor tower, he wasn't quite sure what to do. Actually, he *was* sure what to do. Nod and say yes.

'Help yourself,' 77141 said, eyeing up the bot with the red eyes that hunched in the corner of the control room, trying not to poke a hole in the ceiling with its head. 'I just work here.'

'Most kind,' said the one who'd called himself 'the Doctor', before pulling out some sort of metal pen, making the end of it glow blue, and waving it around.

'Aaah,' he said eventually, peering out of the broken window over sector J. 'Got it!'

'D'you mind my asking,' 77141 asked, trying not to sound at all awkward or confrontational. 'But what exactly is it you're looking for?' He had a bad feeling about this.

'That's the question: what, indeed, are we looking for? I'll tell you that when we find it. Now, before we go a-hunting, it'd be quite useful to know whether any automated defences, orbital weapons platforms, remote-control attack drones,' he waved his hands around vaguely, 'that sort of thing, might be breathing down our necks. It's just that, well, there might be some other people along in a short while, looking for the same thing we're looking for. And since we'd really rather get to it before they do – and trust me, we're the good guys – it'd be nice to have a bit of advance warning about anything that might get in our way.'

The Doctor raised his eyebrows.

'Well,' said 77141 cautiously, one eye still on the bot that the Doctor had called 'Mother', 'um, no.'

'Good!' beamed the Doctor. 'In which case… sorry, what was your name?'

'77141.'

'77141 – strange name. You're not a mechanical are you?'

'No, but if you heard my real name you'd know why a number's more practical.'

'Fair enough. Anyway, 77141, we'll be off. Well, I'll be off. Mother here will keep you company for a while.'

And with that, the Doctor was out of the door and whizzing down to ground level on the tower's lift.

77141 turned his eyes back towards Mother who was

staring at him, her head cocked on one side like a dog wondering whether to attack or not.

'Lovely weather,' said 77141. 'For the time of the year.'

'I've no idea how much of a lead we have on them,' gasped the Doctor and he skidded to a halt beside Boonie, waiting in the shadow of one of Junk's vast piles of rubbish. 'So we'd better be quick. I hope you're beginning to appreciate what an advantage my tinkering with your sensors has given you. We didn't get there in time on Karris – let's get it right this time.'

Boonie gave him a look that suggested he still wasn't convinced. The Doctor pulled out his sonic device and began waving it around.

'This way,' he said, pointing down the row.

As they made their way along the aisles of discarded technology, the night silence only broken by the distant crash of more junk being added and the occasional roar of a rocket engine, Boonie asked about Mother.

'She's keeping an eye on the supervisor for us. If it turns out we need some muscle to get to this segment, we can call her up. Fascinating mechanical, Mother. We had a nice little chat earlier.'

Boonie gave a dismissive snort.

'Told me all about her start in the weapons industry, how she made herself mute, how you rescued her from being scrapped. She's been through a lot. But then you know that.' He threw Boonie a look.

'She told you all that?' asked Boonie incredulously as they walked down the wide street of discarded technology.

'Why not – I'm a good listener. Wouldn't do you any harm to give it a go, either. Just because she can't speak doesn't mean she can't talk.' He paused. 'Or should it be the other way around?'

They came to the intersection of two aisles. Overhead, illumination globes swayed in the gentle breeze, casting dancing shadows at their feet.

'I listen when there's something worth listening to,' Boonie said sullenly.

'You listen when there's something you think you want to hear. There's a difference. Y'know, it's great to have a goal in life – something to get you motivated, get you out of bed in the morning. But sometimes a goal can become an obsession. And obsessions are never good things. Believe me, I've had a few of them myself.'

'You think this is an obsession? Tracking the Cultists, finding out what they're up to? An obsession?'

In the cold light of the lamps above them, the Doctor's eye sockets were unreadable pools of darkness.

'I'm not saying you're not doing the right thing; but it's easy to get carried away with the bigger picture to the point where you can't see the details.' He paused and tipped his head back to look up at the night sky. 'Donna – my friend. Up there.' He gestured at the stars. 'She's a bit like you, only in reverse. Doesn't always see the bigger picture, but you can't fault her on spotting the details.' He grinned at the thought of Donna and her down-to-earth-ness. Well, apart from her stint as a goddess.

Boonie sighed. 'And the point of this is…?'

The Doctor looked back at him, his eyes once more

dark and unfathomable.

'The point is that if you're going to stop the Cult of Shining Darkness then you need to start trusting people a bit more, let them in. And that includes Mother,' he added cryptically. 'Haven't I already shown that I'm on your side? Without me, you wouldn't have been able to plot the trajectory of their ship, detect this segment and get here before them. Without me, they'd have been here before you, grabbed it and scarpered before you'd even arrived. Give me a bit of credit, Boonie.' He grinned. 'Otherwise I'll begin to think that you don't like me very much.'

'Heaven forbid,' sighed Boonie. 'Now stop talking and let's find the segment before they *do* beam it away.'

'Shouldn't be much further,' said the Doctor thoughtfully, consulting his sonic device again. 'In fact…' He took a breath and held out his hands. 'Ta-daaah!' He grinned. 'Always wanted to say that.'

Boonie stared in disbelief at the pile of junk the Doctor was pointing at. At least fifty metres tall, it towered over them like a metal mountain.

'Time we called in the muscle,' said the Doctor. 'And if the mountain can't go to Mother, then Mother will have to come to the mountain.'

Mother was there in under a minute – her red eyes glowing as she lumbered quietly along.

'It's in there somewhere,' said the Doctor, gesturing to the huge cone of discarded technology. 'Now be careful – I'm sure these things were designed to resist a fair bit of battering, but there's no telling how much other stuff they've been buried under all these years. Must admit, it's quite a nifty hiding place for a piece of machinery. Assuming, of course, that it doesn't get snitched by some wandering collector, looking for something glitzy to go over their mantelpiece. These Cultists,' he said, turning to Boonie as Mother began to dig into the pile, 'they must have been well connected once upon a time.'

'They had followers all over the galaxy,' Boonie said, stepping back as a refrigerator came tumbling down the heap to crash at their feet. 'Why?'

'Well, one segment in an art gallery, one in a forest on, where was it – Chao? – one under the surface of a desert world, one here. Can't be a cheap business whizzing all over the galaxy hiding bits and bobs. And you've probably got to pay people to keep an eye on them. Or make them think you're gods, at least.' A sudden thought came to him and he turned to look up at the monitor tower where 77141 was – hopefully – still sitting. 'In fact, now that I think about it, I really should…' His voice tailed off as he began to fiddle with his sonic gadget. After a few moments it gave a low-pitched hum. 'There!' he said. 'Scrambler field.'

'Scrambler field?'

'Should stop the Cultists from just beaming their little treasure out of here. And if I'm right about 77141 up there, it won't be long before the Cultists know that we're here anyway. Wouldn't stop them beaming down somewhere nearby and getting here on foot, but it'll give us a bit more time.'

More rubbish came tumbling down the pile, narrowly missing them. Mother glanced down as if to apologise as she ploughed deeper and deeper into it.

'A bit more time to do what, exactly?'

'Oh, don't worry – I'm not going to stop them getting it. I just want to have a closer look, see if I can work out what it's all for. Soon as I've done that, they can have it.' He paused. 'You sure you know what you're doing, don't you, Boonie? Once the Cult have all the pieces of this thing, they're going to do something with it: build something, find something. Destroy something. Are you sure that's a risk you want to take?'

'You're suggesting that we steal this part, are you?'

'It would stop them. And isn't that what you really want?'

'It might stop them in the short-term. But I bet they have the resources to make duplicates, even if we take this one.' He thought for a moment and shook his head firmly. 'No. They know we're following them. If they go to ground, we might never find them again. This is the way it has to be. They need to keep believing that they're just a bit cleverer than us.'

The Doctor gave a big shrug.

'For the record, I think you're mad, you know that. If you weren't quite so driven by all this, so determined to see it through to the end, you might realise that. But this is your game. Play it your way.' He peered up at where the steel pistons of Mother's hydraulic legs could be seen, sticking out of the pile.

'Any luck?' he called.

'I don't like this,' Garaman said.

'Perhaps the interference is from some piece of discarded equipment on the planet,' Mesanth offered. 'The presence of all that technology is one reason why Junk was chosen for—'

'Garaman!' called Ogmunee from the communications station. 'A message from the supervisor on the planet.'

'Put it through.'

Seconds later, the sound of a very shaky 77141 came through on the speakers.

'However much you're paying me,' he grunted, 'it's not enough to compensate for what I've just been through. Are you listening?'

'With the utmost attention,' said Garaman, weariness dripping from every word. 'What's happened?'

'I've just had visitors.'

'Visitors?'

'A bot the size of a house and a human. They've come for your precious device, I know it. They're in sector J right now. They've done something to the surveillance cameras so I can't see what they're—'

'What did they say? Have you spoken to them?' Garaman cut in.

'Of course I've spoken to them. And you owe me for a new window. And,' 77141 added after a moment, 'a new chair.'

'A new…?' Garaman shook his head. 'We'll be down in a moment. There's interference preventing us from recovering the device from here.'

'That'll be his electronic pen thing,' grumped 77141.

'Whose electronic pen thing?'

'He called himself "the Doctor".'

Garaman's eyes widened.

'Five minutes,' he snapped. 'And you might want to call in some reinforcements. *Big* reinforcements. This might be a tad messy.'

If the two of them hadn't been quite so nimble, Boonie and the Doctor would have been flattened a dozen times over by Mother's careless chucking-out of bits and pieces from the pile. Whilst Boonie gritted his teeth and made sure he stood well back, the Doctor seemed to take a perverse delight in examining every single thing that Mother threw down to them – whether it was (in the Doctor's words) a 'transfluxial rectifier', an ion drive or a coffee percolator.

Boonie still wasn't sure whether to trust the Doctor but, on the evidence so far, he had no reason *not* to trust him. For Boonie, though, that wasn't quite enough. He'd spent two years listening out for Cult activity, scraping together funds and supporters in order to keep an eye on them. He'd been to worlds, governments, federations and alliances across the Andromeda galaxy, trying to persuade them that, just because Khnu em Llodis was dead and her followers scattered, it didn't mean that they weren't still planning something. Boonie had spoken to some of the Cult's ex-members, and he knew what a devious and long-planning bunch they were. Time and time again he kept coming across rumours of a plan – or 'The Plan' as Boonie always thought of it. Something huge, something so big that no one person – perhaps apart from Khnu herself – was privy to all the details.

But there were always people willing to talk if the price was high enough. And using what meagre resources he'd managed to gather, he'd persuaded one or two people to spill at least a couple of beans if not the whole tin. Enough to convince him that if the galaxy's authorities wouldn't do anything about the Cult, then he had to.

And two names that he'd come across, time after time, were Garaman Havati – one of Khnu's chief scientists at the time she'd been killed – and Mesanth, a Lotapareen and another of Khnu's scientists. They'd vanished at the same time, in circumstances equally mysterious. There were no reports of their deaths or their captures by the authorities. But the galaxy was a big place to hide in – or to die in. It was only when word filtered through to Boonie and his little band of Cult-hunters that a Lotapareen answering the description of Mesanth was reportedly showing an interest in a collection of Khnu's unpublished work that alarm bells started ringing.

Months and months of surveillance followed, during which time Boonie accumulated more and more evidence that this was, indeed, Mesanth, and that he was working with others to bring together Khnu's research.

The whole thing was so maddeningly nebulous that Boonie had been close to giving up on more than one occasion. The only thing that drove him on was his conviction that he was right: that the Cult were still active, still planning something – something to do with Khnu's opposition to machinekind's being accepted on the same footing as organics.

And finally – *finally!* – when one of Boonie's spies

reported that Mesanth and brought together a team and had bought a spaceship, he decided that it was time to act.

Boonie, Mother and the rest of the anti-Cultists had followed the Cult ship at a distance as it had entered orbit around the planet Chao. They'd registered the operation of a transmat, bringing something up from the depths of the planet's jungles, before the Cult ship had sped off out into space.

Something – even to this day, Boonie couldn't put his finger on what it had been – told him that this was it. This was the start.

And from then on, for the last month, they'd been on the Cult's tail.

Boonie watched the Doctor scampering about amidst the growing pile of machinery that Mother was throwing down and wondered whether bringing him aboard had really been the right thing to do…

'What's that?' said the Doctor suddenly, tipping his head back as if he were sniffing the air.

For a moment, Boonie had no idea what he was talking about, but as he listened, he heard it: it sounded like distant peals of thunder. Each one was like a distant airplane, crashing into the planet. And each one was accompanied by a shudder through the ground beneath him.

Instinctively, Boonie glanced up at Mother – but she was still somewhere in the pile of junk, pushing bits and pieces of it back out as though she were digging a nest for herself.

'Explosions?'

'Hmmm,' mused the Doctor thoughtfully. 'Could be.' He paused, staring over Boonie's shoulder into the darkness. 'On the other hand…'

Boonie turned at the Doctor's raised eyebrows.

For a moment, Boonie couldn't quite work out what he was seeing. His first thought was that two of the piles of rubbish had somehow come crashing down and were bowling along the ground towards them. But as he watched, he realised what he was looking at.

'Mother,' said the Doctor over his shoulder. 'You couldn't hurry it up a bit, could you? I think we've got company.'

If the Doctor had thought that Mother was a big lass, the two machines bearing down on them were positively *ginormous*!

Side by side, they barely fitted into the wide aisle between the piles of junk. As they drew closer, their steps thumping and vibrating the ground beneath them like miniature earthquakes, the light of the floating globes illuminated them.

The one on the left was built, it seemed, out of a collection of metal spheres of various hues – steel, pewter, bronze, gold – all strung together to make a vaguely humanoid form. It was a house-and-a-half tall but moved with surprising grace. Its head, a coppery-coloured sphere with two dark pits for eyes, tipped slowly downwards as it approached.

The one on the right was altogether stranger: its body was, proportionately, quite slender and could quite easily have been built out of a random assortment of rubbish from the piles around them. Much slimmer than the first

– almost spindly – it had huge, splayed-out feet, not unlike the grabber that had attacked him on the Ood Sphere. But what stood out most were the creature's arms: they were vast, half the size of the thing's body, ending in even bigger, four-fingered hands.

The Doctor had no doubt why the two machines were here.

'They say size isn't everything,' sighed the Doctor, tipping his head back as the two machines drew to a halt twenty metres from them. 'Someone should have told you two.'

'Stop!' boomed the one made of metal balls.

'Yes,' said the other one after a second. 'Stop!'

The Doctor raised his palms.

'Not that I'm one to argue – well, not usually, and not usually with fellas quite as big as you two – but, d'you mind my asking… *why?*'

'Why *what?*' asked the first.

'Why stop? I mean, it's not like we're doing anything bad, is it? Just going through some old junk, looking for a bit of rubbish no one wants. You ever heard of Wombles? Well, think of us as Wombles.'

'Sorry,' said the first one, 'we've got our orders.'

'Yes,' agreed the second. 'And orders is orders.'

'*Are* orders,' corrected the first. 'Orders *are* orders.'

The skinny one turned its car-crash of a head.

'You always have to do that, don't you?'

'What?' thundered the first.

'Correcting my grammar. I don't correct yours.'

'That's because I always get it right. I only do it to help, you know.'

'Well, why d'you always do it in company?'

The first one glanced back at the Doctor and Boonie.

'Hardly company,' the robot muttered.

'It's the principle. I know why you do it, you know.'

'Oh,' said the first, archly. 'Do you? And why's that, then?'

'It's because you're insecure, isn't it? The only way you can make yourself feel good about yourself is to put other people down.'

'That's just rubbish,' scoffed the first. 'What have I got to feel insecure about?'

The skinny robot spread its massive arms wide, knocking the tops off two piles of junk in an almighty crash.

'Where do I start?' asked the other one, as if this were an old, old argument between the two of them.

'Um,' said the Doctor awkwardly, watching the debris tumble to the ground around them.

'Just a moment,' said the first, raising a powerful, blobby hand.

'Fine,' said the Doctor, folding his arms. 'You two go right ahead. We'll just wait here, shall we?'

'Let's talk about this later,' the round one said to its friend. 'We've been told to sort these two out, so let's get this done first, shall we? Save the domestics for—'

'We're not having a domestic,' said the thin one through gritted teeth (or through what passed for teeth in its mighty metal head). 'You always do this as well, don't you?'

The Doctor sighed and planted his hands on his hips.

'Well, it sounds like a domestic to me,' the Doctor called

up. He glanced over his shoulder to where Mother's feet could be seen sticking out of the hole in the side of the pile of junk. More bits tumbled down as she wiggled her legs to get in deeper. 'But I think it's probably important to get these things out in the open, so feel free – go right ahead. We'll still be here when you've finished.'

'Firstly,' said the thin one, 'we're *not* having a domestic, right? And secondly – who on Junk are you?'

'I'm the Doctor, this here is Boonie, and that there – up there, yes, I know you can only see her feet – but that's Mother.'

'A mechanical?'

'Yes,' the Doctor said. 'That OK?'

The skinny robot turned to its friend.

'77141 didn't say there was a mechanical involved.'

'Ahh,' said the Doctor as the penny dropped. '77141 sent you, did he? Now why aren't I surprised at that? What's your names, then?'

'What *are* your—' began the blobby one before the skinny one cut him off.

'Oh do give it a rest, Chuck.'

'So you're Chuck,' interrupted the Doctor. 'And you would be…?'

'I'm Crusher,' said the thin one.

'Nice to meet you,' grinned the Doctor. 'Now, you were saying… 77141 sent you, did he?'

'Trouble in sector J, he said,' boomed Chuck. 'Intruders.'

'Despatch with the utmost force,' added Crusher. 'That's what he said.'

'Oh,' said the Doctor, almost sadly. 'That means you'll be wanting to kill us, won't you?'

Crusher gave a shrug with his entire body, the metal parts screeching and grinding on each other. 'Orders is orders.'

'Orders—' Chuck began but stopped as Crusher turned sharply to him.

'OK,' said the Doctor, not fancying another round of bickering. 'Orders is or are orders. And what is or are those orders, exactly?'

Chuck sounded almost apologetic.

'Kill you all, I'm afraid. Sorry about that.'

The Doctor raised his eyebrows.

'Well, can't say I'm too pleased about it either, but there you go. Orders is – hang on: did 77141 tell you exactly *why* you had to kill us?'

'That lazy good-for-nothing never tells us nothing,' grumped Crusher (and the Doctor winced at the thought of another domestic over his double negative). 'But he *is* the boss…'

'So we do as he says,' Chuck finished the sentence.

'And very right you are to,' the Doctor said. 'D'you mind my asking something? It's about your names.'

'Well, I'm Crusher,' said the skinnier one, 'cos I crush stuff up.' He raised his hands and flexed the immense fingers with the creak of metal on metal and the hiss of hydraulics.

'And I'm Chuck,' added the fatter one, 'cos I chuck stuff into the sun. Not the good stuff, mind,' he added, as if the Doctor might think he were just a vandal. 'Just the rubbish that no one wants.'

'Into the sun, eh?' said the Doctor admiringly. 'That must take some skill.'

'Oh it does,' agreed Chuck, flexing his fingers. 'People think it's easy – they think it's just brute force, overcoming gravity and all that. But it's not. There's a lot of maths involved – otherwise, it just goes into orbit or messes up the system. Gotta get it just right.'

'And crushing isn't as simple as it sounds,' added Crusher, clearly feeling left out.

'Not as hard as chucking,' said Chuck.

'Well, maybe,' agreed Crusher awkwardly.

'Ladies, ladies,' cut in the Doctor. 'Or gentlemen, gentlemen. I'm sure you're both very special and very unique, and me and Boonie here are very impressed. So 77141 has given you orders to come and crush – and chuck – us, has he?'

'Fraid so,' said Chuck, almost regretfully.

The two of them took a mammoth step forward and the ground shook. Crusher raised his hands in front of him and flexed his fingers.

'Who's first, then?' he asked.

'Probably me,' the Doctor said. 'But before you start with the crushing and chucking, I don't suppose it would make any difference if I told you what we're doing here, would it?'

'Shouldn't think so,' replied Chuck.

'But you could always try,' Crusher added, clearly trying to be reasonable.

The Doctor glanced at Boonie who, throughout

the whole conversation, had hovered nervously in the shadows.

'You ever heard of the Cult of Shining Darkness?'

'*Those* nutters?' laughed Chuck.

'The anti-machine nutters?' added Crusher. 'The mechanet was full of stories about them a couple of years ago. Didn't they fall apart or something?'

'The woman leading them died, didn't she?' asked Chuck.

'That's them,' the Doctor agreed, wincing at his own grammar and hoping it didn't set Chuck off again.

'So what have they got to do with you?' asked Chuck. His voice suddenly went very growly and low and he bent forwards. 'You're not with them, are you?'

'Oh no!' exclaimed the Doctor. 'No, not at all – in fact, we're on the other side. The goodies, as it were. Ask Mother up there – well, when she comes down.'

Chuck straightened up slowly, but clearly wasn't convinced.

'But your 77141,' the Doctor went on slowly. 'Now he's a different matter.'

Chuck and Crusher exchanged glances.

'You're kidding,' said Chuck. '77141?'

The Doctor reached down and dragged a finger across some of the junk at the bottom of the closest pile before holding it up to show them the muck on it.

'How long is it since sector J had a good clean-out?'

'Must be at least two years,' Chuck said, and Crusher nodded.

'And is that at all unusual for Junk?' asked the Doctor

casually.

Crusher and Chuck looked at each other again.

'Well,' said Crusher, 'now you come to mention it, it is a bit odd.'

'Most stuff round here's on a one-year rotation,' Chuck added. 'You know how quickly technology gets out of date. If it's not been reclaimed or recycled in a year, me and Crusher usually get to work on it, crush it up real small and send it on a one-way cremation trip.'

The Doctor nodded thoughtfully.

'So the fact that this particular lot of junk hasn't been touched for so long is a wee bit suspicious, you'd say?'

The two robots swapped glances again.

'Y'know,' said Crusher slowly. 'You might – and I say *might* – be onto something there. Masher, over in sector E, was going to bring the remains of a Hajaveniakii stasis chamber over here, but 77141 made him carry it all the way over to T. He wasn't happy, I'll tell you.'

'So,' said Chuck, straightening up. 'Let me get this right, Doctor. You're saying that that lazy lump up in the control tower is somehow in league with these daft culty types and they've paid him to keep people away from this sector, are you?'

'Well, either paid him or he's doing it out of the goodness of his heart.'

'Paid,' said Chuck. 'Lagacteons don't have hearts.'

'Or goodness,' added Crusher.

'I don't suppose you've got any proof?' asked Chuck. 'I mean, it's a bit of an accusation to make, isn't it, regardless of whether he's a lazy, fat, heartless lump or not?'

The Doctor sighed.

'No proof at all, I'm afraid. Not unless you count the fact that he's clearly so worried about what we're doing here that not only has he sent you two, but he's sent *those* as well.'

As he spoke, the Doctor raised an arm and pointed back down the aisle.

Illuminated in the cold glow of the light spheres overhead, a tide of crawling, creeping, scuttling machines was flowing towards them.

Boonie squinted into the darkness: it was as though the ground itself were wriggling and shifting.

'Now tell me that's normal,' the Doctor said, and Boonie realised he was talking to Chuck and Crusher.

'What's he playing at?' whispered Crusher – although his whisper was louder than most people could shout.

'Your boss clearly doesn't trust you to get the job done,' said the Doctor. 'He's called in reinforcements.'

'Has he indeed?' said Crusher in a low, serious voice. 'Well, we'll see about that. There's union rules about this sort of thing.'

'We're not *in* a union,' Chuck pointed out.

'Well, maybe we should be.' Crusher raised his head and swivelled it through 180 degrees until it was facing back towards 77141's tower. 'Oi!!' he bellowed in a voice like thunder that rolled on and on and on. 'Boss! What's going on here?'

Seconds later, amplified by 77141's speakers, the reply came back.

'I gave you two bots a job to do, and instead you're standing around gassing. You can't carry out simple instructions? Fine! Then let these bots do it instead!'

There was a grinding, crunching groan from inside Chuck, and Boonie saw how he clenched his blobby hands.

'I've told him about that,' he muttered, gears whirring inside him. 'We're *not* bots. We're mechanicals. How many times…?'

'Calm down, pet,' said Crusher. 'He doesn't mean anything by it.'

'Don't tell me to calm down,' grunted Chuck. 'And yes he does mean something by it: he means he's too lazy to take any notice when I say I don't like being called a *bot*.'

And with that, Chuck bent low and swiped his right hand across the ground in the path of the dozens of service and maintenance robots that were scuttling towards them, sending them tumbling and clattering into each other, bouncing end over end like kicked marbles.

'He's not going to like that,' warned Crusher with a worried shake of the head.

'Stuff whether he likes it or not. Let him have his way and, before you know it, we'll be on the scrapheap – *literally* – and these… these *appliances*,' he spat the word, 'will be doing our jobs for us.'

But the little robots just kept on coming, legs clicking, caterpillar tracks whirring.

Boonie backed towards the Doctor who was looking worriedly up at Mother's feet, still sticking out of the heap behind them.

'We need to get out of here, Doctor,' he whispered, hoping that Crusher and Chuck's hearing wasn't good enough for them to pick up his words.

The Doctor's face fell, like a child who's been told his holiday had been cancelled at the last minute. He was clearly enjoying it.

'If the service bots don't get us,' Boonie continued urgently, 'those two will. It's not worth the risk.'

'Oh, it's always worth the risk, Boonie,' the Doctor suddenly grinned as, emboldened by Chuck's stance against the little robots, Crusher joined in, sweeping his freakishly long fingers along the ground and sending dozens and dozens of the little 'appliances' bouncing end over end. 'This is what living's all about – get rid of the risk, what's the point of it all, eh?'

The two of them seemed forgotten by Crusher and Chuck as they clearly started to enjoy their battle against the little machines. Wave after wave of them clattered and clicked their way across the ground and over the bases of the piles of junk around them, like a plague of mechanical insects. But as they did, working as a perfect team, Chuck and Crusher cleared them out of the way, almost effortlessly.

'We're gonna get the sack for this,' said Crusher – and glanced at Chuck.

'I know,' Chuck replied, laughing. 'But you know something – I reckon it's worth it!'

And with that, Chuck gathered up a handful of wriggling, squirming appliances, took aim, and lobbed them with frightening accuracy in the direction of 77141's observation tower. Boonie held his breath for a moment – until he heard the sound of multiple crashes and bangs. As he watched, the lights of the tower wobbled and began to move, describing a slow arc as it began to topple.

'Bullseye!' cried Chuck, punching the air.

With a final, echoing crash, the tower hit the ground – and to everyone's surprise, floating out of the darkness, there came the sound of cheers. Not just from one mechanical, but from dozens, all over the place.

'Sounds like you two are heroes,' commented the Doctor.

'77141 always was a fat, useless lump of lard!' laughed Crusher as he squeezed another handful of appliances until their cogs fell out. He tossed the motionless remains onto one of the piles at his side.

'Now…' Crusher dusted the remains of the broken machines from his fingers and bent low over the Doctor and Boonie. 'What we gonna do with you little Squidgies?'

'Squidgies?' said the Doctor.

'Sorry,' apologised Crusher. 'It's what we call you organics. No offence.'

'None taken, Crusher.' The Doctor paused. 'Can you tap into records of recent planet-to-ship communications?'

Crusher glanced – a little shiftily, Boonie thought – at Chuck, who was still at work flinging the last wave of robots into the air.

'Not officially, no.'

'OK, well, say you were to unofficially tap into them. Just, y'know, theoretically.'

'Yeeesss,' said Crusher, dragging the word out.

'And,' continued the Doctor, pulling a face and kicking the ground with his toe, 'say you were to check whether a certain ship currently in orbit had been speaking with 77141…'

'Go on.'

'Would one of those communications be about making sure that we didn't get our hands on—'

'He's right!' cried Chuck suddenly. 'I've found the message! The scheming, bloated, sack of—'

Chuck was cut off by the sight of Mother, emerging from the junk mountain and holding something aloft – something huge and circular. She held it in one hand as if it weighed next to nothing as she clambered carefully down, sending a shower of debris clattering down the heap as she did so.

'Crusher, Chuck – meet Mother. If you're in any doubt about our credentials, ask her – she'll tell you.' The Doctor checked his wristwatch. 'But you're going to have to make it quick: they're going to be here any minute,' he said, motioning for Mother to lay the device on the ground.

'So what's that, then?' asked Crusher, stomping on the last, few straggling appliances.

'That's what we want to find out,' the Doctor said gleefully, bounding over to the segment.

In the dim light from the floating globes overhead, even Boonie could see that the device had received a considerable battering. The wheel-shaped casing was dented and scraped. Hardly surprising considering the mass of junk that had been piled on top of it.

'Is it damaged?' he asked anxiously.

'Well, give me a chance to examine it and I'll tell you.' The Doctor rolled his eyes. 'Look, if you want something to do, go and check how 77141 is. He looked a tough old thing and he may well have survived the fall. If he has, he might already be telling the Cult what's happening. They might be planning on coming down with some reinforcements. Take Mother with you – you might need her.'

Boonie was torn: he didn't fancy leaving the Doctor here with the device, but, equally, he didn't want to be caught by the Cultists. 'Go on,' said the Doctor when Boonie didn't move. 'Shoo! Go on!'

'What are you going to do?'

'I'm going to see if it's damaged – and if I can work out what it does.'

'You're not going to sabotage it, are you?'

The Doctor frowned.

'Sabotage it? Why would I do that?'

'To stop the Cultists.'

'Oh, that. Nah. You know, you've piqued my curiosity, Boonie. I'm almost as curious as you are to find out what it does. And like you say, if they don't get this one to work, they may just go to ground again. And much as I've loved my trip to your galaxy, I really can't hang around for ever to help you track them down again. Now *go*!'

With a shake of the head, Boonie beckoned Mother and the two of them headed off to the monitor tower.

'You're sure you don't need our help?' asked Crusher.

'You two have been wonderful,' the Doctor grinned up at the machines. 'A credit to machinekind everywhere.'

'Hear that?' said Chuck proudly.

'We like to do us bit,' Crusher added.

'*Our* bit,' Chuck corrected him.

'Here we go again,' sighed Crusher with a shake of the head.

'Lovely couple,' the Doctor said to himself with a smile as he watched them go, still bickering. 'Right, you little beauty,' he said with glee as he hunkered down next to the segment. 'Let's see what you're made of, eh?'

He pulled out the sonic screwdriver, checked that it was still emitting the scrambling frequencies that he'd set it to earlier, and activated the secondary circuits. Gingerly, he began to play its blue light over the surface of the segment…

'Doctor.'

He looked around, wondering where the voice had come from.

'Boonie?'

'No, Doctor.'

Cautiously, he stood up, the sonic still in his hand. There was no sign of anyone – not Boonie, not Mother. No one. And then he saw it. It had been hidden by the random piles of machinery thrown down by Mother and the broken bits of appliances left by Crusher and Chuck, but once it moved he saw it.

It was a robot, about the size of a large child. Its upper body was a scratched, pale blue cube, its lower body an inverted pyramid from which sprouted two segmented legs ending in flat, circular feet. Two similar, flexible arms

extended from the sides of the cube. A small screen was set
into the front of the body near the top, glimmering bluey-
white. It had no visible head.

'I don't think I've had the pleasure,' he said charmingly,
reaching out a hand. But the robot remained where it was,
ten metres away.

'I'm using this servitor as a conduit to speak to you,' the
voice said. It sounded surprisingly lively, but the Doctor
had no idea whether that was its real voice, the voice of
whoever was speaking through it, or just a disguise.

'Who are you?'

'You don't need to know that.'

'Oh. OK. What *do* I need to know?'

'You need to know that if you attempt to interfere with
the device at your feet, in any way, that you will not see
Donna Noble alive again.'

The Doctor clenched his jaw.

'I don't take kindly to threats,' he said sourly. 'Particularly
not ones directed against my friends.'

'Then don't take it as a threat, Doctor,' the voice said, its
bouncy nature sinisterly at odds with its words. 'Take it as
a promise. Interfere with the segment and Donna dies.'

NINE

'How do I know you'll honour your word?' asked the Doctor.

'You don't. But if you do anything to the segment then you can be sure that we *will*. This is not your fight, Doctor.'

The Doctor sighed and stuck his hands in his pockets, kicking at a bit of scrap on the ground.

'Now, y'see, threatening Donna is the fastest way to make sure it *is* my fight. You really haven't thought this one through, have you? If you'd just given Donna back to me, then things might have been different.' He shook his head ruefully. 'But you had to go and do the threatening bully-boy bit, didn't you? I mean, assuming you are a bully-boy and not a bully-girl. There're plenty of those around. It's not big and it's not clever.'

The Doctor stopped as he caught a brief flare of white light from one of the side aisles.

'The recovery party beaming down, eh? Hope Donna's

amongst them. I want to make sure she's OK before I agree to anything.'

And to hammer home his point a little more, he took a step up onto the segment and began jumping up and down on it.

'Hello!' he said cheerily as two figures – a muscled black man with a grim, angry face and a thin, blonde, humaniform robot – stepped into the light. He looked around in mock puzzlement. 'No Donna?'

As if in answer, there was another flash of light and a slightly bemused Donna materialised a few metres to the side of the new arrivals. She squinted in the darkness, getting her bearings, before she spotted him.

'Doctor!'

'Hello again!' he grinned, hands in pockets, still jumping up and down on the segment like a child full of tartrazine. 'We're really going to have to stop meeting like this. People'll begin to talk. Especially with you being a goddess an' all! "Too good for him!" they'll be saying.'

'They wouldn't dare,' laughed Donna.

Donna started to head towards him, but the man stepped forward with an outstretched hand to stop her. She pulled an apologetic face at the Doctor.

'Looks like I can't come out and play just yet,' she said.

The man indicated that Donna should stay where she was, and then he and the blonde robot crossed to the Doctor and stood a few feet from where he'd finally stopped his bouncing.

'You've set up some sort of interference field, haven't you?' asked the little, boxy robot chirpily.

The Doctor smiled and pulled out the sonic screwdriver, the tip of which was glowing a gentle blue.

'Turn it off and step off the segment.'

Keeping an eye on Donna, the Doctor jumped down; the man and the robot came and stood right next to the battered artefact.

'The interference field, Doctor,' the little robot reminded him.

'Oh yes.' He fiddled with the screwdriver for a moment.

'Good,' said the robot. 'Thank you. Goodbye, Doctor. Let's hope our paths don't cross for a while. I'd hate to have to be the one to inform you of Donna's death. One never knows what flowers to send, does one?'

'What?' called Donna, not understanding what the little robot was on about.

'Donna!' called the Doctor, stepping back from the segment as he felt the hairs stand up on the backs of his hands.

'What?'

'Catch!'

And with that, he flicked the slider on the side of the sonic and sent it spinning through the air in Donna's direction. As he did so, he waved cheerily – and jumped back up onto the segment, just as the snowy glow of the transmat enveloped it, the muscle man and the blonde robot.

And him.

Reflexively, Donna caught the sonic – in time to see the Doctor and the rest of them vanish.

'Oh,' said the little blue robot, surprised. 'I wasn't expecting that.'

'What happened?' came a voice – it was a young white kid with a nose-stud, sprinting towards them, and a massive great robot, thundering along behind him.

'The Doctor – he's gone,' said Donna, still trying to work it all out.

'Gone?' said the boy. 'Where?'

'Garaman's ship. They've beamed him up.'

Suddenly, there was a clattering noise, and the little robot fell over, its arms and legs flailing about all over the place.

'*Garaman?*' said the boy, ignoring it. 'Garaman Havati?'

'You know him?' asked Donna, still trying to work out what had just happened. It was all going too fast for her to keep up. But the boy didn't answer. He touched something on his lapel and then pulled a face.

'Kellique says there's some sort of interference field here, stopping us from beaming up.'

Donna held up the sonic screwdriver.

'This?'

'The Doctor's device? That'll be it – turn it off, quick, otherwise they'll be long gone. We need to beam up to our ship, quickly!'

Confused and dazed – but still a little suspicious – Donna slid the slider on the sonic and the glow faded. The boy touched his lapel again.

'What about that one?' Donna asked, pointing to the robot that had spoken to the Doctor earlier. 'It was having some sort of argument with the Doctor. I think it might be one of theirs.' It still lay motionless, looking just like another piece of the scattered debris that surrounded them.

'Fine,' the boy said. 'Come on – oh,' he added to the robot looming over him. 'Mother, can you…' He pointed to the little robot.

Silently, the giant robot strode over and picked it up in its hand. It looked like a doll. The two of them stood alongside Donna, and the boy tapped his lapel again.

'You know something,' said Donna with a sigh as she felt the familiar tingle of the transmat. 'I'm getting bl—'

'What's *he* doing here?' shouted the muscled guy once the disorientation of the transmat journey had passed.

The Doctor had already jumped off the segment and was peering around the purple room aboard the ship.

'You should let Boonie have the number of your interior designer,' he said. 'Very chic!'

'Hold him!'

Realising that resistance would probably just get him injured – or worse – he let the blonde robot grab his wrists and restrain him.

'Ow!' he yelped. 'You don't know your own strength, you don't. Problem with your feedback receptors?'

The man didn't answer, but caught sight of something bulging in the Doctor's pocket. Without so much as a by-your-leave, he reached in and plucked it out.

'What's this, then?' he asked, holding up a shiny red sphere, the size of a tangerine.

'Oh…' said the Doctor casually. 'That. You wouldn't be

interested in that. Trust me. If you just let me have it back, we'll say no more about—'

'This is not your ship, Doctor,' Ogmunee interrupted him. 'Don't presume to lecture me on what I would and wouldn't be interested in here.'

He examined the sphere, turning it over in his hands as he tried to make sense of the blocky black markings on its surface.

'What is it?'

'Something bad, I imagine,' replied the Doctor, hoping that Ogmunee wouldn't try to open it. He'd fail, of course – the Doctor had tried himself until he'd realised what it was. 'I mean, it's not likely to be a Christmas bauble is it, looking like that?'

Ogmunee just raised an eyebrow and tucked the sphere awkwardly into his own pocket.

'I'll have a look at it later.' He sighed theatrically. 'So you're the Doctor, are you?' asked the man, looking the Doctor up and down with distaste. 'Donna's friend.'

'And you would be…?'

'Ogmunee,' answered the man. He looked around the room, suddenly realising that something was missing. 'Where *is* Donna?'

'Ahh,' said the Doctor a little sheepishly. 'That would be me. I lent her the sonic screwdriver. Hope she looks after it. Doesn't start using it to clean her teeth or anything. It's got three settings for—'

The door hissed open and a short, officious man with blond curls trotted in. His mouth dropped open, literally, when he saw the Doctor. He bounded over, looking the

Doctor up and down as if were about to eat him – or have him shot.

'This is the Doctor,' said Ogmunee.

'What's he doing on board?'

'It didn't seem fair that Donna should have all the fun,' the Doctor said, wriggling in the grasp of the robot. 'So I thought we'd do a bit of a *Wife Swap*. I must say, you've got a much snazzier ship – but don't expect me to do cleaning. *Hate* cleaning. Not too bad with the ironing, though.'

The little man's eyes narrowed.

'So you're a friend of that useless little amateur Boonie, are you?'

'Oh, don't underestimate Boonie,' the Doctor warned. 'He might be a bit of an amateur, his ship might be falling apart, but he's a lot smarter than you give him credit for. And dedicated. And an ounce of dedication's worth a whole load of competence. What's your name, anyway?'

'Not that it matters to you, but I'm Garaman – Garaman Havati.' He looked up at the Doctor superciliously. 'Ring any bells?'

The Doctor thought for a moment. Someone called Garaman Havati *had* been mentioned in the records that Li'ian had showed him. He pulled a face and shook his head.

'Not even a tinkle. Should it?'

It clearly annoyed Garaman that Boonie hadn't mentioned his name – but then why should he have done? According to Li'ian, they had no idea which of the Cultists were on board the ship. Well, apart from one...

'How's Mesanth, by the way?'

Garaman's eyes widened. And then narrowed as he clearly realised that, although Mesanth was important enough for the Doctor to know about him, he, Garaman, wasn't.

'You know him?'

'Only by reputation.'

Garaman's lips tightened.

'You'll meet him soon enough.'

He glanced at Ogmunee and the robot.

'Bring him to the bridge. I want to find out what Boonie and his little friends know.'

Fearing that his arms were about to be wrenched from their sockets, the Doctor let himself be dragged from the room.

This was getting ridiculous, thought Donna. It was like she and the Doctor were working different shifts and only got to see each other at tea time. And what was more, Boonie's ship stank.

'Sorry we lost the Doctor,' Boonie said. 'It seems he used that device of his to block the Cultists' transmat of you but was outside its range himself. At least you're in safe hands now.'

'Am I?' Donna had yet to be convinced. She glanced up at the hulking silver machine – apparently called 'Mother' – standing behind her. The blonde supermodels on board Garaman's ship might have been a bit scary, but this thing was *terrifying*.

'And what d'you mean, "the Cultists' transmat"? If you're the good guys, why was the Doctor so keen to get away from you?'

'Think about it this way…' This was Li'ian, an elderly woman, who seemed slightly out of place amongst the rest of them. 'If he'd thought *we* were the bad guys, he wouldn't have made sure you ended up in our hands, would he?'

Donna had to concede that that made a certain sense.

'And who are these Cultists? You mean Garaman and Mesanth?'

Li'ian glanced at Boonie.

'They didn't tell you about the Cult of Shining Darkness?' she asked Donna.

'Why would they?' sneered Boonie. 'They're hardly going to advertise the fact that they belong to a Cult.'

'No reason why they shouldn't,' said Li'ian. 'They're not exactly ashamed of who they are, are they?'

Donna raised her hands for them to stop.

'Look,' she said firmly. 'I've just come from one ship where everything was more mysterious than a Miss Marple. I'm not about to walk into a Hercule Poirot. Just tell me what the hell is going on!'

She glared, first at Boonie and then at Li'ian. She ignored the slight whine from the robot towering over her. It was giving her a very strange look – well, as strange as a face like a jet-engine part could manage.

'Garaman and Mesanth are leaders of what remains of a—'

Boonie stopped as there was a grinding, mechanical noise from the middle of the room.

They all turned to see the little robot they'd brought up from Junk, flailing its bendy arms and legs, trying to right itself. In seconds it was sitting up on the rusty floor, the screen on the front of its blue, boxy body flickering.

'Oh my,' it said in a chipper voice and gave a shudder before turning towards them.

On the screen, the cartoon image of a little man's face appeared. The mouth moved in exaggerated astonishment as the short pen-strokes of eyebrows went up.

'Oh my…'

'Mother…' Boonie said, gesturing at the robot as it swivelled its upper body to look around the room. In seconds – and with surprisingly little of the earthquake-style ground-shaking that Donna had expected from such a hulk – Mother was at the robot's side, looking down on it. It tipped back so that it could look up: the sight of Mother, towering over it, must have scared the thing half to death, thought Donna.

'Oh…' it said again.

'Yes, yes,' snapped Li'ian. 'We get the point. You're shocked. Now why were you arguing with the Doctor?'

'What?' The face on the robot looked genuinely surprised – but then, thought Donna, that damned paperclip that popped up on her computer when she started writing a letter looked genuinely *helpful*. 'Who?' the robot added, twizzling around again. It tried to get up, but Mother's firm, metal paw came down on its top, pinning it to the floor.

'The Doctor,' said Donna grimly. 'The man you were talking to about my death and what flowers you'd send to my funeral.'

'The who, the what?' The robot flailed its arms around,

slapping them ineffectively against Mother's hand. 'Oh my, this is all very unexpected.'

'Oh, sunshine,' said Donna, crouching down so that her eyes were on a level with the robot's screen. 'You have *no* idea what other unexpected things we can come up with if you don't start telling us the truth.'

The cartoon face flashed to astonishment.

'Of course I don't, otherwise they'd hardly be unexpected would they? Although, of course,' his face went all thoughtful, 'events could be both unexpected and yet not unknown, since "expected" could be seen to apply to their timing as well as to their nature, couldn't they?'

'What?' said Donna.

'I said—'

'I know what you said. Now look, either you start telling us who you're working for, or... or...' Donna floundered around, trying to think of something to threaten the robot with. 'Or I'll get Mother here to crush you into a ball of scrap so small that you won't even be able to get a job as a doorstop.'

There was a sharp intake of breath from just behind her. It was Li'ian. Her hand was halfway to her mouth in an almost comic gesture of concern.

'It's just a robot,' said Donna, rolling her eyes. 'If necessary, we'll take it apart, circuit by circuit...'

Donna stopped at the expressions of outright horror on the faces of Boonie and Li'ian. She turned sharply as even Mother joined in with a deep, electronic groan.

'Barbarian,' whispered Boonie.

'Come again?' Donna still wasn't getting it.

'I'm finding it hard,' said Boonie grimly, 'to believe that the Doctor spoke so highly of you. How dare you come aboard my ship and start threatening people like that? What kind of a civilisation do you come from?'

'Threatening people?' echoed Donna. 'I'm not threatening people, for god's sake.' She gestured at the robot, its cartoon face a picture of amazement – eyes and mouth wide open. 'It's. A. Robot.'

Donna sat back on her haunches – how could she make it any clearer? What was wrong with these people?

'Don't you want to know who it's working for?'

'What's your name?' Boonie asked the robot, ignoring Donna.

'Weiou,' the robot said.

'Right, Weiou. Donna here says that you threatened the Doctor. Is that true?'

'Me? Threaten the who?'

The robot looked around, looking genuinely confused.

'Just a mo,' he said, screwing up his cartoon eyes tightly. His screen face went dark for a fraction of a second.

'What's he doing?' asked Donna suspiciously.

'Connecting to the mechanet,' said Boonie. 'Resynchronising his clock.'

Weiou shook his face as though he were clearing away cobwebs.

'Oh my,' he said, eyes wide. 'I've been hijacked! I'm missing eight minutes and thirty-seven seconds.'

'You're saying you can't remember what happened to you?' Donna wasn't sure whether it was telling the truth. 'What's the mechanet, then? Some sort of internet for robots?'

Weiou nodded.

'I'm missing eight minutes and thirty-seven seconds,' it repeated, as if this were the most unbelievable thing ever.

'Weiou,' said Li'ian gently. 'Can you come with me? I can run a couple of diagnostics on you – see if we can work out what happened to you.'

Donna glowered at the woman: she was treating the robot like some sort of dizzy elderly relative when they should have been taking a screwdriver and a spanner to it. There was little she could do – clearly they were more concerned about not upsetting the thing than trying to get the truth out of it.

'Meanwhile,' said Boonie, as Mother helped the robot to its feet, 'we need to get after the Cultists' ship. Kellique says the Doctor's modifications to the sensors mean we're still tracking it.' He threw a sneering glance at Donna. 'You'd better come with me,' he said, turning away and heading for the door. 'The Doctor clearly sees something in you, although god knows what.'

And before Donna could respond, Boonie swept from the room.

'Doctor,' Donna whispered to herself. 'I hope you're having as much fun as I am...'

A chair had been brought into the control room of Garaman's ship, bolted to the floor, and the Doctor tied to it. The blonde robot stood silently at his side.

'Why did you get yourself beamed aboard our ship, Doctor?' asked Garaman, hands on hips.

'Oh, you know how it is – change of scenery and all that. Besides, I've been hearing so much about you – you and your little cult – that I thought it was about time I met you face to face.'

At the mention of the word 'cult', Garaman's eyebrows rose and he glanced towards the door that had just hissed open.

'This,' Garaman said to someone out of sight, 'is the Doctor, Donna's friend.'

'Garaman,' sighed a warbly, fluty voice. 'I'm seriously beginning to wonder about you. Is there any need to tie him up like this? Have you learned nothing from the way you treated Donna?'

Into view came a three-legged, three-armed lizard, its head shaking sadly.

'I'm Mesanth,' the creature said, looking at the Doctor with wide, unblinking eyes. They were slate grey, the pupils diamond-shaped.

'Ahh! The infamous Mesanth!' said the Doctor, smiling cheerily.

'Infamous?' Mesanth looked alarmed.

'Well, you know what Oscar Wilde said about being talked about…'

'No,' Mesanth replied simply. 'What did he say?'

'That it was better to be talked about than *not* to be talked about. Pleased to meet you. I'd shake your hand but, as you can see…' He glanced down at his hands and wiggled his fingers.

'Oh, for goodness' sake, Garaman – untie him,' exclaimed Mesanth. 'What good is this going to do? Which bit are you going to threaten to remove, hmm? How about his head?'

The Doctor felt momentarily alarmed. He was quite fond of his head – and he was pretty certain that if they chopped it off it wouldn't grow back. Although if it did, maybe it'd be the ginger one he'd always wanted. Go quite nicely with his friend the Ginger Goddess.

'You deal with him, then!' spat Garaman, waving his hand dismissively. 'We're reaching Sentilli. I can do without the distraction.'

With a bitter shake of his head, Garaman waddled off to the bridge's control chair.

Mesanth set about untying the Doctor with two of his three-fingered hands.

'Ahh!' exclaimed the Doctor, rubbing his wrists. 'Thank you!'

'My apologies,' Mesanth said humbly, waving the blonde robot away. It went to stand quietly near the door. 'Garaman tends to be a little overeager.'

'Oh, don't be too hard on him. I like enthusiasm. And I'm sure he's got enough on his plate, what with collecting all these segments and finishing off Khnu's plan – what?'

The look on Mesanth's face was priceless: his fingers flexed and writhed suddenly, like agitated snakes.

'How do you…' began Mesanth. 'How do you know about Khnu?'

'It's all there in the records,' replied the Doctor. 'Well, not all. That's the thing: there's no mention of what, exactly, she was up to. That's why I thought it might be good to come aboard and have a chat to the people who're actually doing it, y'know, "living the dream". So to speak.'

He stretched his arms and looked up at the lizard.

'So…' He beamed. 'Where shall we start?'

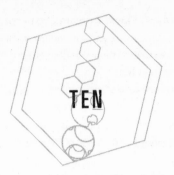

TEN

Donna was beginning to wish she'd stayed with Garaman and Mesanth: the former might have threatened to break her little finger, but they hadn't shown the outright hostility to her that this lot had. And all because she'd tried to get information out of Weiou.

Although they hadn't locked her up, they seemed to have assigned Mother, the hulking great steel robot, to look after her. Which was as good as.

'Why do they call you Mother, then?' she asked, sitting in a room that they laughingly called the cafeteria. 'Oh, sorry – forgot: you don't talk, do you?'

It was frustrating: just seconds away from being reunited with the Doctor, they'd been snatched apart again, and now she had to get to know a whole new set of weirdos. The way they talked about the Doctor suggested that they'd gotten on well, but she suspected that whatever goodwill the Doctor had built up with them had well and truly been lost by her. She didn't understand it: their attitude to robots was seriously screwy.

As she ate something that tasted like a cheese sandwich (but looked like fish pie), Mother stood there silently, glowering down at her.

'D'you have to stare at me while I'm eating?'

Mother inclined her head slightly. It was as though she were trying to figure her out, like she'd never seen a human before (and *could* a robot be a 'she'? How did that work, then?).

'So what did the Doctor say about me?' she asked, pushing aside the remains of her lunch. 'Gorgeous? Witty? Stylish in a practical and down-to-earth sort of way?'

Mother just stared – but then, as the only other crew member in the room left, the robot glanced around in a curiously human way before kneeling on the floor on the other side of the table. Donna wondered if Mother were about to whip out an engagement ring and propose to her.

Suddenly, a tiny spot of pink light appeared in the middle of Mother's chest, and a pale, flickering rectangle sprang up in the air between them.

>DONNA. THE GINGER GODDESS.

As red as Mother's eyes, the words were sketched out in front of her.

'How d'you know ab- oh!' She smiled. 'The Doctor told you.'

>I WAS THERE.

'You were? Where?' It suddenly hit her. 'It was you that pushed that rock, wasn't it?'

>YES.

'Well, thank you,' Donna said. 'Without you, we'd probably have been burned at the stake. Well, Mesanth and Ogmunee would, at any rate.'

>YOU'RE WELCOME.

Donna stopped as, overlaid on the words was a moving image – it was *her*! The image showed her approaching whatever camera the video had been taken with, her mouth moving silently as she looked over her shoulder, clearly arguing with someone. The picture froze and then repeated, looping round and round.

'Where's this from?' she asked.

>YOU TRIED TO HELP MECHANICAL ZB2230/3 ON KARRIS.

'Oh!' It all came back to her. The bimbot. 'That!'

>WHY?

Donna was thrown for a moment.

'Well, it was hurt.'

>ITS LIPANOV RATING WAS 23. IT WAS NOT SENTIENT. YET YOU TREATED IT AS IF IT WERE.

'Its what?'

>LIPANOV RATING – A MEASURE OF MACHINE SENTIENCE. MECHANICALS WITH A LIPANOV RATING OF 40 OR MORE ARE GENERALLY CLASSED AS SENTIENT. THOSE BELOW ARE NOT.

The words scrolled off the edge of the screen area faster than Donna could read them.

'Whoa!' she said. 'Back up there a bit, sunshine.'

Mother's words scrolled back round again, slower this time.

'And what's yours – your Lipanov thingy?'

>80.

'Oooh,' said Donna, trying to sound impressed. 'A right little brainbox!'

>IT DOES NOT INDICATE INTELLIGENCE – ONLY SENTIENCE, SELF-AWARENESS.

'Right,' Donna said carefully, not at all sure that she understood the difference.

>WEIOU RATES 68 AND YET YOU ATTRIBUTE LESS SENTIENCE TO HIM THAN TO ZB2230/3. IS THAT BECAUSE OF HIS APPEARANCE?

'Um,' said Donna, starting to lose track.

>BECAUSE HE IS LESS HUMANIFORM, clarified Mother, YOU ASSUME THAT HE IS LESS SENTIENT. WOULD THAT BE ACCURATE?

'What?'

>YOU JUDGE HIS WORTH BY HIS APPEARANCE.

Donna's mouth almost fell open. She remembered the conversation she'd had with Mesanth about the difference between the bimbot and the door.

'What are you saying?' she demanded. 'Are you saying what I think you're saying?' She felt her face redden. 'Are you calling me a *racist*?'

>THAT WOULD BE TO JUDGE BY RACE. YOU JUDGE BY APPEARANCE. THAT IS DIFFERENT.

Donna closed her mouth tightly. And then opened it again, ready to rebuff Mother's words with something clever and sharp and witty.

But there was nothing there.

Mother had accused her of judging robots by what they looked like, not by how sentient they were: how different was that from racism? And if she couldn't argue against the first bit, how could she genuinely, hand-on-heart, argue with the second? She *wasn't* racist. She knew she wasn't. But no matter how she turned it over in her head – as Mother knelt and watched her, silently – there was something horribly inescapable about the robot's conclusion.

'Where I come from,' Donna started carefully, chewing at her bottom lip and carefully avoiding Mother's gaze, 'things are different.' She summoned up the courage to look up into Mother's implacable face. 'We don't have…' She nodded towards the machine. 'Robots. Not like you. Not like Weiou.' She paused again, struggling to find the right words. 'You lot – all of you Andromedans – you're so… so *weird*. No offence,' she added hastily. 'Not weird, exactly. Just strange. Different. Back home in Chiswick, the closest I'd ever get to a conversation with a machine is shouting at the photocopier.' She shook her head again. 'It's only natural to see something that doesn't *look* human and doesn't *act* human and to assume it doesn't *think* human, isn't it?'

>IT IS UNDERSTANDABLE, agreed Mother.

There was a long silence.

'It doesn't make it right, though.' Donna said quietly. 'Does it?'

>NO. BUT WE ARE ONLY AS IGNORANT AS WE CHOOSE TO BE.

Donna gave a bitter little laugh. At herself.

'Meaning it's up to me how much I learn about other people? Now you're just being nice,' she said.

>IMPLYING THAT YOU ARE IGNORANT IS NICE?

'Believe me, it's better than what you could have called me. I'd say sorry, but sorry doesn't really cut it, does it? Not over something like this.'

>WE ARE ALL PRODUCTS OF OUR PROGRAMMING, OUR EDUCATION, said Mother. IT IS HOW WE TRANSCEND THAT PROGRAMMING THAT DEFINES US. I WAS CREATED AS A WAR MACHINE. I HAVE CHANGED. WE CAN ALL CHANGE.

Donna chewed on a fingernail, recalling the attitudes of Mesanth and Garaman and their absolute certainty that they were right. How could people so right be so *wrong*?

'But robots can't *feel*, can they? I'm not being horrible, but…' She struggled for the words. 'But robots are just *things*, aren't they? I mean, they're built, made out of metal and circuits and stuff. They're not alive. Not really.'

>YOU MAY NOT BE MADE OF METAL, BUT YOU'RE STILL 'MADE OF STUFF'. WHY DOES IT MATTER WHAT THE CONSTRUCTION MATERIAL IS?

'But Mesanth says that robots are just mimicking thinking and feeling.'

>AND HOW DO YOU KNOW THAT *YOU* ARE NOT JUST MIMICKING THINKING AND FEELING?

'Because I *know* I'm not.' Donna tapped the side of her head. 'It's all in here. I *know* what I feel.'

Mother raised a steel hand and repeated the gesture, tapping the side of her head.

>ME TOO.

Mother had given Donna a lot to think about, but she wasn't going to be allowed the luxury of time to herself to get it all straight in her head. Boonie called the two of them through to the control room, where Weiou was running around like an overexcited child, chatting to the other robots (even the little service ones that, Mother had assured Donna, were so low on this Lipanov scale that they barely counted as food mixers).

'He's innocent,' said Li'ian. 'Someone – someone with a pretty good knowledge of robotics and communications systems – hooked into him and used him as a mouthpiece. I've checked his memory out and he's just got a blank space there.'

'Garaman?' suggested Donna, feeling vaguely traitorous for suggesting it, despite the conversation she'd had with Mother.

'Who else?' glowered Boonie.

Weiou caught sight of Donna and came over, his cartoon face a picture of distress.

'Sorry,' he said.

'It's OK,' said Donna, giving him a little pat – that she hoped didn't seem too patronising. 'It's not your fault. Sorry I was such a bully. I was just worried about the Doctor.'

'S'OK,' said Weiou. 'Still,' he added, his upper body turning as he gestured to the control room and its occupants. 'Wow!' His eyes went wide. 'You've no idea how exciting all this is, you really haven't. I mean, all this jetting about space and chasing bad guys and stuff – it's probably all in a day's work to you lot. But I've spent all my life on Junk – cataloguing, sorting, organising.' He made a typing gesture with his fingers. 'This is the kind of life some of us can only dream of. What's next? Where are we going now?'

Donna had to smile – he was like a little puppy. And whether Mesanth was right, and he was just imitating enthusiasm – or Mother was, and it was all genuine – Donna couldn't help but be infected by it.

'There are two possible systems on the hyperspace trajectory that Garaman's ship took,' Kellique said, and a transparent, holographic display sprang up in the air at the front of the control room. 'The Sentilli system, which has a black hole as its primary, and Pew, which has a binary star. If they're looking for an inhabited world, Pew is the more likely, although all sixteen of its planets are in very erratic orbits. Sentilli has thirty-six planets, but they're all pretty much washouts as far as life goes because of the nature of their sun.' She shrugged. 'Until they emerge from hyperspace, we won't know for sure. Another hour and we'll have a better idea.'

'Meanwhile,' said Boonie, turning to Donna, 'I think we need to talk.'

Donna nodded.

'I'm really, really sorry about what I—'

'No, no,' Boonie cut in. 'Not that. That's something we might have to discuss later. I mean Garaman and his little band. We need to know anything that might help us work out what they're up to – anything they might have said, no matter how insignificant. Take your time – let's see what we can come up with.'

'I was quite warming to your friend Donna,' Mesanth said.

'She had some… strange views, but I think she was an essentially good person.'

'Can we talk in the present tense, please,' said the Doctor. 'Hopefully, she's still alive. And yes, she *is* a good person. Why, what's she been saying?'

'Her experiences with mechanicals are interesting,' Mesanth said, and the Doctor noticed how he smelled of fish and lavender. Not the most usual odour, but certainly not the most unpleasant that he'd encountered.

'Told you about the robot Santas, did she?'

Mesanth nodded. 'She gave the impression that your galaxy has far fewer mechanical civilisations than ours.'

'It would seem so, yes,' the Doctor agreed. 'But then both galaxies are so huge that it'd be a bit unfair to draw conclusions from the little bits of them that I've seen. Wouldn't want to seem like I'm generalising. Never a good thing, generalising.' He winked at the joke, but Mesanth didn't seem to get it.

'Of course,' agreed Mesanth (a tad overeagerly, thought the Doctor). 'But you must agree that there has always been friction between mechanicals and organics.'

'Oh, always is such a big word. It's on a par with "every" and "never" and "they're all a load of lazy, scrounging gits and they should get back to their own planet" isn't it?' He smiled at Mesanth, but his eyes were hard and humourless. 'What were we saying about generalising?'

'Ahh,' said Mesanth after a moment's pause. 'You're a promechanical.'

'Am I? Really?' The Doctor sounded quite excited at the suggestion. 'I like to think of myself as pro-*humanity*, whatever shape that humanity comes in.' He raised a hand as Mesanth began to speak again. 'And if you're going to start arguing with me that mechanicals aren't really alive, then I'll stop you here, save you the time. Stop thinking of someone as being like you and it means you can start treating them differently. And usually treating them *worse*. That's the kind of thinking that leads to segregation and prison camps, isn't it?'

'Facts are facts,' Mesanth said.

'And arrogant, opinionated nonsense is arrogant, opinionated nonsense and I really don't have time to listen to any more of it. I'd much rather you told me about this thing that you're collecting the parts for.'

Mesanth's hands began to flex again.

'The way I see it,' the Doctor continued, breezily, 'is that if you genuinely believe all this tosh, then you ought to be quite proud of it, and more than willing to go on about it at length to me. All this organic supremacist stuff's a bit old hat, isn't it? "We're better than you cos we're made of goo rather than metal," etc, etc. You seem like quite an intelligent fellow – d'you *really* believe it, or is it just something to do at the weekends? Like re-enacting military battles or getting drunk on cheap cider. You can't *really* believe it.'

'You haven't experienced what we have,' Mesanth said. 'Our galaxy is being overrun with machine intelligences. Given enough resources, they are capable of reproducing at a much greater rate than most organics.'

'Granted,' agreed the Doctor. 'But they *haven't*, have they? How long have you had peace here? How many centuries have organics and non-organics lived, side by side, with barely a war or a skirmish? How much have organics and non-organics contributed to each other's cultures?'

'The point is,' Mesanth said firmly, 'that that can't continue for ever.'

'Why not?' The Doctor leaned forward, his face right in front of Mesanth's. 'It's worked pretty well up to now, hasn't it? If the people of my galaxy could see yours, they'd be astounded at the way you've all gotten on up to now. Wouldn't you rather be seen as leaders in interstellar peace and harmony than yet another galaxy of bickering, scrapping kids?'

'It must seem very simple to you, as an outsider,' said Mesanth. There was a hint of frustration in his voice, the Doctor thought. 'You have no understanding of the issues involved here.'

'Oh,' retorted the Doctor, 'I think I have. Anyway, I'm not going to convince you, and you're not going to convince me, so why not just tell me what it is you're up to, what Khnu's grand plan was, and then I can go back to Donna and we can leave you to get on with it?' He grinned, but there was an edge to his smile.

Mesanth eyed him warily – when suddenly Garaman's voice squeaked over the intercom.

'We're entering the Sentilli system,' he said. 'All crew to their stations. Repeat, all crew to their stations.'

'Oh,' said the Doctor, crestfallen. 'And you were just about to explain your plan to me. Don't you just hate it when that happens!'

ELEVEN

The Doctor watched, appalled at his own stupidity, as the assembled device rotated in space, just half a kilometre from the hull of the *Dark Light*. Now that the four segments were stacked upon each other, the Doctor could see how they formed a cylinder – obvious, really, with hindsight. But then wasn't everything? Each segment rotated independently as the whole device turned silently until one end was pointing towards the black disc of Sentilli.

'You're going to open up a black hole!' he said slowly and turned to Garaman. 'I should have guessed.'

'Why should you have guessed?' asked Mesanth.

The Doctor shrugged.

'Well, the bit you collected on Uhlala contained some rather nifty dimensional resonance coils; the one on Karris had some sort of zero-point energy converter in it, from the sketchy readings I picked up; and the one on Junk gave all the signs of being a spatial dephaser. Put 'em all together and you've got the galaxy's biggest can-opener.'

He grinned at his own cleverness. 'Normally, I'd say that's brilliant. But I've got a feeling that it's not going to be brilliant for anyone apart from you.'

Garaman laughed dryly.

'Can-opener. I like that. There was a point,' he said, 'where I thought you were going to work out what it does. But now it doesn't matter.'

'Oh, I think it matters a great deal,' said the Doctor ruefully. 'But I don't think there's much I can do about it, is there?'

Garaman just smiled.

'So what's in there? An army of organic beasties just waiting to be awoken and take on the might of your galaxy's machine intelligences? Or is it some kind of refuge? A little Shangri-La where you and your organic supremacist friends can live without worrying about your paranoias? A Little Andromeda, if you like. A paradise free of machinekind?'

Garaman said nothing. Instead, he gestured at the screen.

At one edge, closest to the *Dark Light*, was the tiny, jewel-like shape of the can-opener, sparking blue lightning dancing around it. And at the other, away in the distance, was the jet-black disc of Sentilli, the black hole at the heart of the system, visible only because it obscured the stars behind it.

'Activate,' whispered Garaman and Mesanth tapped at the control panel.

The glow around the can-opener began to grow, deepening to an almost painful purple as it shifted out of the range of the ship's scanners, before the device seemed to turn completely black.

'Dephasing has begun,' said Mesanth, and the Doctor caught the look of almost Messianic glee on Garaman's face.

'Watch, Doctor,' said Garaman. 'Even though you've been a pain in the backside, I have to admit that it's quite nice to have a witness for this moment.'

The Doctor squinted as Garaman called for Mesanth to increase the scanner magnification. The image leaped, picking out the edge of the black hole from where, silently, like a sleek ocean liner emerging from fog, something huge was rising from the depths of the darkness.

It was vast, and the resemblance to an ocean liner grew as the vessel exited the black hole and headed towards them: its main body was slim and pointed, like a sharpened grain of pale green rice. Numerous antennae and struts jutted from it at right angles to it, giving it a spiny appearance. Towards the rear, the density of the spines increased greatly, making it look not unlike an enormous loo brush, thought the Doctor. As it headed towards them, tiny pinpricks of light began to spring up on its surface.

'We call it *The Torch*,' said Garaman in a whisper.

The Doctor humphed. 'You do love your light-and-dark metaphors, don't you? *Shining Darkness*, *Dark Light*, *The Torch*. What next, *The Candle in the Wind*? Still, I'm impressed. Must have taken you years to build this – especially in secret.'

'Oh, it did. Years and years and *years*. Keeping it secret was the hardest part, employing – ironically – teams of primitive robots to build it.'

'And then wiping their memories when they'd done their part.'

'Exactly. If only they'd had real sentience, they might have realised that they were orchestrating their own destruction.'

'Their own genocide would be closer to the mark,' the Doctor corrected grimly, but Garaman just smiled tightly.

The Torch, as Garaman had called it, pulled away from Sentilli and began to slow as more and more lights came on across it.

'Just received a signal,' Ogmunee said suddenly, glancing at the Doctor.

'From?' asked Garaman – before his cherubic mouth formed into an 'o' of realisation. 'Safe?' he asked – and he too looked at the Doctor. There was something the two of them weren't sharing with him. Ogmunee nodded and smiled.

'Right!' said Garaman suddenly. 'One more thing to attend to before we get on with the business at hand.'

Ogmunee was standing by the weapons systems control panel, a cold smile on his face that suggested he knew exactly what was coming.

'Have the weapons charged to full,' Garaman ordered. 'Time to put Boonie and his robot-lovers out of our misery, I think.'

'What're you doing?' the Doctor demanded as Ogmunee turned back to the controls and began operating them.

'You didn't think I'd leave that rag-tag little band of no-hopers a chance to interfere any more, did you?'

'They can't hurt you,' the Doctor said levelly, keeping

one eye on Ogmunee. 'Let them go.'

'I don't think so,' Garaman said. 'It's not over till it's over, and I'd rather not take any chances. Not so late in the game.'

The Doctor drew himself up.

'You do realise that if you kill them, I'll have no reason not to do everything in my power to stop you, don't you?'

Garaman raised his eyebrows wearily.

'You're suggesting that if I let them live you'll let me finish what I came here for? I hardly think that's likely. You know, I'd quite like to have you killed now, but Mesanth and his conscience would probably have something to say about it. And I could do without him throwing a hissy fit. Besides, I'd rather see the look on your face when you find out what's actually aboard *The Torch*. Call it professional satisfaction. Or showmanship.'

He glanced over at Ogmunee who nodded.

'Ready,' he growled.

'Say goodbye to Donna, Doctor,' Garaman smiled before nodding at Ogmunee. 'Fire,' he said, and Ogmunee pressed the button.

Boonie's ship shuddered and from somewhere deep inside it, Donna heard a rumble that echoed on and on. She gripped the edge of Boonie's chair to steady herself as the floor vibrated beneath her.

'What was that?'

'They've fired on us,' Kellique said, disbelief written all over her face. 'They've fired on us!' She checked the displays again. 'Damage to drive unit. Decks three and four are heavily breached. We're venting atmosphere.'

The Sword of Justice lurched again and Donna was thrown against the wall. Mother swayed on her feet, the hydraulics in her legs hissing as they compensated.

'Can we seal off those areas?' shouted Boonie over the sound of a warning siren. The bridge was plunged into a blood-red gloom as emergency lighting cut in.

'Too late,' Kellique said after a moment. 'We've got coolant leakage from the drive – it's eating its way through the hull. Estimated time until we lose hull integrity – eleven minutes, give or take.'

Boonie clasped his hands to his forehead.

'No!' he said through gritted teeth. 'No!'

'Boonie,' said Donna, trying to remain calm. 'Life boats, life pods, whatever you call 'em. D'you have any?'

'What?' He looked at her as if her words were nonsense. 'Yes, yes.'

'Good – get everyone into them. Crew, robots, the lot. If the ship's going to blow, they'll stand more chance in them, won't they?'

Boonie just stared at her, paralysed by everything going on around him. Donna could see the despair in his eyes.

'Oh my,' said Weiou, his cartoon eyes wide with shock. 'Donna's right, you know. Bagsy me first!'

'Shut up!' snapped Boonie, running his fingers through his hair. Donna was reminded, momentarily, of the Doctor, and she wondered what he was doing right now...

'Kellique – give the order!' shouted Donna. 'Get everyone off.'

Kellique looked to Boonie for confirmation: for a

moment, Donna thought he was going to go to pieces, but eventually he nodded, grim-faced. Kellique grabbed a microphone and began bellowing orders at the ship's crew, ordering them to the escape pods.

'Whew!' said Weiou. 'That's a relief – so what are we waiting for?'

'We're not waiting for anything,' Boonie said. 'We're staying here – I'm staying here.'

'You heard what she said,' Donna shouted, grabbing his arm as yet another explosion, somewhere deep in the bowels of *The Sword of Justice*, threw them around. She stumbled against Boonie's chair, catching her hip, painfully. 'The ship's going to blow. What use is staying here? It's not like in a film you know. You won't be standing proud on the prow as the ship sinks with everyone thinking how noble you were.' She grabbed his wrists and pulled him round until he was looking at her. 'You're going to *die*.'

Boonie licked his lips feverishly, pulling away from Donna.

'Not alone, I'm not,' he said. He raced over to Kellique. 'Do we have any sort of drive power?'

'Only attitude thrusters, why?'

Boonie considered for a moment, rubbing his forehead.

'It's enough,' he said. 'Get them online. If we're going down, we're taking them with us.'

'We're what?' shouted Donna above the wail of the sirens.

'That ship,' Boonie said, jabbing his finger towards the screen on which they could see the spiky behemoth that had emerged from Sentilli. 'That's their big weapon. It's what they've been working towards all these years. And I'm damned if they're going to get their hands on it.' He fixed his eyes on Donna as he gave the order to Kellique. 'Ram it,' he said. 'This ship's the only weapon *we* have left, and we're going to use it!'

'Stop it!' roared the Doctor, rushing towards Ogmunee.

At a single gesture from Garaman, the blonde humaniform robot stepped in and wrapped its arms around the Doctor, hugging him in a vice-like grip to its chest. The Doctor was powerless. If he'd had his sonic screwdriver, there might have been a chance that he could have deactivated it, scrambled its circuits. Something. But he didn't, and his arms were pinned to his sides.

Suddenly, the door slid open and Mesanth came trotting in.

'What's happening?' he demanded to know of Garaman. 'You're firing the weapons – why?'

'Our little nemesis, Boonie,' he said – and the Doctor could see the annoyance on his face at Mesanth's arrival. 'Time to put an end to him.'

'You can't,' Mesanth said, his face a picture of confusion. 'There are organics aboard that ship.'

'Barely,' Garaman growled. 'Besides, you didn't really think that our whole plan could be achieved without any loss of life – organic life – did you?'

Mesanth waved his hands helplessly.

'No, but… You said there would be no unnecessary deaths. You said there'd be no need to destroy their ship.'

Mesanth sounded close to tears.

'Well then, just think of this as the first in a series of sad, but ultimately necessary, casualties.'

'Tell him, Mesanth,' grunted the Doctor, struggling to breathe in the grip of the robot. 'Tell him to let them go – they can't do any harm now. You've probably already crippled their ship. They might even be dead. Call off the attack. You claim to care about life, about organics. Prove it. Make him stop.'

Mesanth opened his mouth and looked at Garaman.

'After all this time,' Garaman said, almost reluctantly. 'After all this planning... You want to let a bit of sentimentality ruin everything.'

'But... but what if the Doctor's right? They can't do anything to interfere now.'

'You want to take that chance, Mesanth? Really?'

'Garaman,' Ogmunee cut in carefully.

'What?'

'The ship – Boonie's ship. It's moving.'

Garaman turned sharply to the main screen and Ogmunee brought up an image of it.

'They're trying to escape,' Garaman murmured, a cruel smile playing across his cherubic lips.

'No,' Ogmunee said, frowning. 'No, they're not. They're going the wrong way. They're heading *inwards*.'

The Doctor realised what was going on before anyone else did.

'Oh dear!' he said, tugging against the robot. 'Seems they're not so helpless after all!'

'What are they doing?' said Garaman, slowly

approaching the screen as *The Sword of Justice* picked up speed. Tiny flickers of light from the attitude thrusters showed that the ship didn't have much motive power – but it had enough.

'They're heading for *The Torch*,' Ogmunee said, almost disbelievingly.

Mesanth gave a little warble of alarm.

'They're going to ram it,' he whispered.

'Oh no they're not,' Garaman said through gritted teeth. 'Target them again – this time we're going to finish them. For good.'

'Emergency pods are detaching,' Kellique said, counting them off as they left, spiralling away into the darkness. 'The crew are all safe.'

Donna had no idea whether the escape pods would be able to make their way home, or whether they'd just float around in space until they ran out of air and power. But it was better than sitting around on *The Sword of Justice*, waiting for it to hit the Cultists' supership. Weiou flapped his hands helplessly.

'We should be going,' he said, over and over. 'We should be going. I didn't sign on for this. Oh my.' Weiou paused as he caught sight of the display in front of Kellique. 'The escape pods – they've all gone.' He did a comedy gulp.

'Weiou,' said Donna brightly.

'Yes?' The little robot looked up at her.

'Shut up.' She turned back to Kellique. 'How long until we hit that thing?'

Her mouth was dry and her pulse racing. There was

every chance that they were going to die, but something – maybe it was the adrenalin, maybe just the rush of everything that was going on – kept her going through the panic that she could feel battering away at the back of her mind. She fought it down again as it rose up, threatening to overwhelm her and turn her into a screaming ball of mush, cowering in a corner. *It's what the Doctor would do*, she kept telling herself. *It's what the Doctor would do.*

'Eight minutes,' Kellique said, and Donna could hear the tremor in her voice.

'Eight minutes,' Donna repeated, more to herself. 'Right. Can the ship be left on autopilot to ram that thing?'

Kellique nodded.

'Good! Do what you have to – lock the controls, whatever. We're not done yet.'

'But all the escape pods have gone,' protested Weiou. 'All of them. Every last, single one—'

'Weiou,' said Donna gently, crouching down next to the robot. 'D'you remember what I threatened Mother would do to you when you came aboard? Well if you don't shut up, I'll do it myself. We still have one escape pod.'

'We don't,' protested Kellique. 'Weiou's right – they've all gone.'

'Oh no they haven't,' said Donna with a smile. 'Come on!'

Donna hovered in the doorway as Kellique set the controls on auto.

'I hope you know what you're doing,' glowered Boonie as Donna waved him and the others out into the corridor.

'Trust me,' Donna grinned, gripping the doorframe as

another tremor shot through the ship. 'I might not *be* a doctor – but I've learned a few things from a pretty good one.'

It took them almost five minutes to make their way back through the deserted, broken ship. The main corridor was blocked by fallen debris, but Mother made light work of it, lifting the twisted beams and wall panels out of the way as if they were cardboard and polystyrene. Weiou was usually the first to scoot through the gaps Mother created, until Boonie pointed out that they had no idea what lay beyond every corner, after which he huddled in the middle of the little band.

'Nearly there,' Donna said as they reached their destination: the ship's small cargo hold. It was only then that Boonie realised what she was up to, and his normally miserable face broke out into a grin.

'If you ever want a job on my ship – well, on my *next* ship—' he began, but broke off as he saw the look on Donna's face.

She was staring through the grimy porthole of one of *The Sword of Justice*'s bulkheads into the cargo hold. A bulkhead that was sealed shut. A bulkhead that, by all rights, should have given them access to the TARDIS. The *ultimate* escape pod.

All Donna could see through the thick glass was a bit of floor and then nothing. Nothing but empty space: the room where Boonie had stowed the TARDIS had been blown clean open in the attack, and the TARDIS, their only way off the dying ship, had gone.

TWELVE

'I am in *so* much trouble,' she whispered. She'd only gone and lost the TARDIS, hadn't she? 'Apart from the fact that we're all going to die, of course,' she added.

Another explosion rocked the ship, the distant screech of torn metal galvanising her into action. She turned to Kellique.

'Right,' she said. 'No TARDIS. You're *sure* there are no other escape pods? Not even an emergency one…?' Donna shook her head. 'What am I on about: *all* escape pods are emergency ones, aren't they? And you're sure the transmat is down?'

Kellique nodded.

'What about pod eight?' said Boonie suddenly.

'Eight's been out of action for months,' Kellique reminded him.

Donna jumped at this. 'Out of action? Why?'

'The locking mechanism's seized up – the external clamps have become vacuum welded.'

'So what you saying? That it'd work if you could get it unwelded? Never heard of WD-40? Never mind,' Donna added at their blank faces. 'Can't we wiggle it loose? Cut it free?'

'Not from inside, we can't, and the EVA suits are all gone. And besides, they're four-person pods – and there are five of us. And Mother's not exactly compact…'

Donna ran her hands through her hair – and was thrown against the wall as the ship bucked beneath their feet again. *Think, Donna*, she told herself. *Think!*

And then she caught sight of Mother.

Mother!

D'uh!

'You sure this is designed for four people?' grumped Donna as she squeezed through the tiny hatch into pod eight alongside Boonie and Kellique. Arms and legs and elbows were everywhere. 'Four midgets, maybe.'

'Oi!' squeaked Weiou as he, too, tumbled into one of the padded seats set around the inside of the little vehicle. 'Nothing wrong with midgets!'

Kellique shook her head as she buckled up. 'You sure this is going to work?' she asked Donna.

'No,' replied Donna sharply. 'Of course I'm not sure this is going to work, but if you've got a better idea, now might be quite a good time to tell us about it. Mother!' Donna craned her neck to see Mother, still outside the pod's hatch. 'You ready?'

Mother nodded silently – and with a dull clang the hatch sealed itself.

'Well,' said Donna, sitting back and smiling. 'Isn't this nice? Very cosy. How long will it take her, d'you think?' she added as they were rattled by another – much bigger, much closer – explosion from somewhere on *The Sword of Justice*.

'Now there's no one left on board,' Boonie said, checking his watch, 'Mother can just open the bulkhead and get out that way. If this is going to work, we'll know about it soon. One way or another.'

Donna took a deep breath. She only hoped she wasn't condemning them all to death in the escape pod. The realisation that, even if they could get the escape pod free, there wouldn't be room on board for Mother had been the trigger: in a flash Donna had realised that, of course, Mother didn't *need* air. (Neither did Weiou, but Weiou didn't have the brute strength that Mother did).

The plan was obvious in its simplicity. Maybe *too* obvious – which made Donna a bit suspicious of it: the three humans and Weiou could get in the pod, Mother could clamber outside the ship and free the docking clamps before hitching a ride on the outside of the pod. Kellique had checked that the pod's thrusters were still working, so there'd be no problem in steering it towards the space station that had emerged from Sentilli. Obviously, there was no way to tell what kind of welcome they'd receive when they got there; but it had to be better than staying to be blown up.

All four of them started as a sudden harsh, metallic clanging sounded through the pod's hull. And then another. It was like something monstrous was trying to tear its way in.

'Sound worse than it is,' said Kellique, registering the look on Donna's face. 'Trust me. Even if I'm *not* a doctor.' She smiled grimly.

There were more clangs – and then an ominous grinding sound.

One final clang and a creaking, tearing groan that seemed to drag on for ever before it ended in silence.

'She's done it!' cried Kellique. 'That's the clamps disengage- whoa!'

The pod suddenly lurched, and it was only the fact that they'd all belted themselves in that stopped them from being flung around the cramped interior. The lights suddenly dimmed to red.

'What is it with the red lights on spaceships?' complained Donna. 'It's not like we *need* a status report from them, is it? Oh God, I feel…'

'Gravity's offline,' said Kellique.

'Never have guessed,' said Donna, trying to keep a grip on the contents of her stomach.

'Whoo!' cried Weiou excitedly. 'Hang on everyone – here we go!'

Anyone watching from outside would have been clenching their fists in anticipation: a line of explosions was bursting out from the skin of *The Sword of Justice*, rippling along it, twisting and warping the vessel's hull, heading towards the tiny blister of emergency pod eight. And, hugging itself tight to the pod was Mother, spreadeagled on the top of it and clinging on for dear life.

With a flare of blue light, the pod's thrusters fired up

and it popped free of the ship, as the wave of explosions swept across the mothership. Slowly, but building up speed rapidly, the pod jetted out into the cold blackness of space, a tiny, silhouetted spot against the raging inferno it was leaving behind.

In mute disbelief, still held in the robot's steely embrace, the Doctor could only watch as *The Sword of Justice* slowly accelerated through the Sentilli system, on a collision course with *The Torch*.

It was a brave – but futile – hope.

Streams of gas and fuel trailed out behind the pathetic, battered wreck of a ship, turning it into an artificial comet. All across its hull, lights were going out. Tiny explosions erupted all over its surface, sending clouds of sparkling debris out into space. The absence of a sun made it hard to make out any details, but the *Dark Light*'s sensors were enhancing the image, showing the death throes of the ship in all their sad glory.

Donna…

The Doctor could only hope that she'd either escaped in a lifeboat, or that she'd had the sense to take shelter in the TARDIS. Assuming that his lovely little blue box hadn't already been blown out into space.

'Target acquired,' said Ogmunee with relish, catching the Doctor's eye and flashing him a cruel, toothy smile.

'Finish it,' Garaman said, almost wearily. 'We've got more important things to be getting on with.'

From the side of the screen, a thick pencil of deep purple light sprang up, stretching away into space, skewering *The*

Sword of Justice through its flank like it were a kebab. For a moment, nothing happened – the ship continued to move, allowing the beam to slice it open along its side. And then a cascade of explosions started up, glowing boils of gas erupting into the darkness, one after another. Finally, the little ship could stand no more. As the purple ray reached the tail of the ship, its innards began to glow – first a dull red, and then upwards, faster and faster, through yellow and white through to an eye-searing blue. And then the screen flared white and the Doctor closed his eyes.

Donna.

THIRTEEN

'This must have cost a small fortune,' the Doctor whispered in awe as they made their way through the darkened space station. He was in a grim mood after the destruction of Boonie's ship.

The Torch, it became clear as soon as Garaman, Mesanth, the Doctor and the blonde robot had transmatted aboard it, was more than just a spaceship.

'Several fortunes,' said Garaman proudly. 'And none of them small. You'd be surprised how many philanthropists are behind us, even if they can't come out and openly admit it.'

'And what have you promised these *philanthropists*? What do they get out of whatever little nutjob scheme you've got planned?'

'Satisfaction, Doctor. The satisfaction of living in a galaxy where organic beings are where they should be – at the top of the heap.'

It was like strolling through a vast warehouse: huge,

open spaces, unlit and echoey, were all around them. The ceiling was so high it was lost in the darkness. And there was a cold fustiness about the air. Like a tomb, unopened for centuries. The smell of metal and electricity surrounded them, and their footsteps clanged and echoed on the floor as they walked.

'You're going to keep me guessing, aren't you?' said the Doctor as they passed through into another chamber the size of an aircraft hangar. Several spangly new spaceships sat side by side, silent, waiting to be used, their hulls the same pale green as *The Torch*.

'About what? The purpose of all this?' Garaman chuckled. 'Yes, I think I probably am. Humour me. If it helps, this –' He waved a hand around him '– is all a bit of overkill really. Before her death, Khnu was constantly scared that she'd be caught, brought to trial on some trumped-up charges by the promechanicals. She wanted to make sure that if she ever had to go into hiding that she'd have somewhere decent to continue her work. To spend the rest of her life, if necessary.'

'So she designed her own prison, did she?' The Doctor was unimpressed.

'Oh, far from it. Just think how sophisticated this place must be to hide itself inside a black hole, Doctor, without being crushed into the singularity at the heart of it. It's a masterpiece – the perfect bolt-hole. Not a prison.'

'You say tomato,' sang the Doctor without much enthusiasm. 'I say to-*may*-to. A prison's a prison, no matter how chintzy the curtains are. Still, she'll never get to find out now, will she?'

'Sadly,' said Garaman – although his face showed anything but sadness, 'she won't, no.'

'You're not going to tell me that it was you that engineered her accident, are you?'

'Doctor!' Garaman looked genuinely shocked. 'Of course not! I worshipped that woman. She was a genius. Without her, none of this would have been possible.'

'Hmmm,' murmured the Doctor. 'But at least now you get it all to yourself, don't you? And what about you, Mesanth? What d'you think of your new home?'

'It's not a home,' Mesanth said primly. After the destruction of *The Sword of Justice*, some of the fire seemed to have gone out of him, and he'd hardly spoken two words since they'd beamed aboard *The Torch*.

'Still worrying about all those dead people, are you?' the Doctor said mildly, with just the hint of an edge to his voice. 'The ones that died because of you. The ones that burned, out in space. *Those* people.'

'Their deaths were unfortunate,' Mesanth said, avoiding looking at him, 'but necessary.'

'That's right,' said the Doctor. 'Just like Garaman said. You keep telling yourself that. Doesn't make it true, but it might make you feel better. And whilst you're thinking about deaths, necessary or otherwise, remind yourself that they aren't going to be the last.'

'What?'

'Oh, there'll be more deaths to come, mark my words. There always are with people like Garaman in charge. Whatever little plan you two are cooking up, whatever revolution you're bringing to the galaxy, it's going to involve death. Lots of it. Buckets and buckets of it. Organic and inorganic, human and machine. And I wouldn't be surprised if a few energy and gas beings get caught up in the crossfire.' The corner of his mouth tightened. 'Bad business, war. No one comes out of it unscathed.' He paused. 'Believe me.'

'It's necessary to break eggs,' said Garaman, 'to make omelettes.'

'Oh,' retorted the Doctor, rolling his eyes. 'That one. I'd have thought someone of your intelligence could have come up with a slightly better justification than that.'

'I don't need to justify myself to you.'

'So why *are* you? Feeling a bit guilty? Trying to make sure Mesanth here stays on-side right until the end? And what's your part in all this, Mesanth? You just along for the ride? I don't know much about your species – where are you from, by the way?'

'I am a Lotapareen – from Lota.'

'Well, I don't know about the Lotapareen, but I'm surprised that you've got much in common with Garaman. Well, apart from the hatred of machines. It's a great thing, hatred: sits very well with fear. And that's what all this is about, isn't it? *Fear.* Fear of difference, fear of the unlike, fear of things you don't understand. Fear of things that aren't like *you.*'

'I don't fear machines,' Mesanth replied levelly as they stepped into the wire cage of a lift that began to sink into the depths of the space station. 'I simply want organic life – *true* life – to take its rightful position in the galaxy. I have nothing against machines.'

'Of course not,' mocked the Doctor gently. 'Every home should have one. They're great at building things and picking up heavy weights, but they really need to know their place, don't they? Don't want them getting all above themselves. Where does it stop, though, eh? First it's machines. Then what?' The Doctor threw at glance at Garaman. 'Got a thing against tall people, maybe, Garaman?' He pulled a dismissive face. 'Get rid of 'em, eh? Oh, and then there's thin people – don't like thin people, do we? Ship 'em all off to an island where they can be with their own kind. And reptiles. What about reptiles, eh, Garaman?' He looked Mesanth up and down. 'Shifty lot, reptiles. Like it hot and dry, not like us *humans*. Can't be trusted, I say. Let's get rid of them, too, shall we?'

The Doctor saw Mesanth's eyes widen, just momentarily.

'And before you know it,' finished the Doctor, folding his arms, 'all we're left with is a universe of Garamans. Little, scared, power-mad Garamans. All the same, all with a chip on their shoulder, all blaming everyone else for how the universe has turned out.' He leaned forwards and peered down at Garaman. 'And when you've done all that, and you look around and find that the universe isn't any better after all, what d'you do then, eh?'

'It won't work,' said Garaman through gritted teeth. 'Trying to set Mesanth against me. We've worked together long enough to know what we both think, what we believe. A few clever-clever words from you aren't going to upset that.'

'Are they not?' The Doctor sighed. 'Oh, well, I won't

bother, then.'

He plunged his hands into his pockets and stared at the ceiling as, in silence, the lift fell along the length of *The Torch* towards the control centre.

As they dropped through the roof of the control room, the Doctor mused on how much effort – how much *machine* effort – must have been involved in constructing the station. It was the size of a small town, and to build something so huge without anyone outside suspecting, was an enormous achievement. But like so many achievements, it would be how it was put to use that would ultimately define it, and he wasn't hopeful. He hadn't said anything to Garaman and Mesanth yet, but the spines at the rear of the station looked suspiciously like Bishop converters, designed to extract energy from black holes. What could they need so much energy for…?

They stepped out onto the floor of the control room, and lights flickered and flared around them. They were on a broad, circular platform, darkness receding on all sides. Curved banks of instruments and controls were arrayed around them, each in its own little pool of light. It felt more like a museum than a command centre.

'Nice, don't you think?' said Garaman.

'As hunks of metal go – no offence,' he added to the supermodel robot that hovered at his side, 'it's very nice. But what's it *for*?'

'Liberation!' said Garaman dramatically. 'Think of it as the pearl in the oyster of this station.'

'Abandoned your light-and-dark metaphors, have you?

Don't blame you really – they were getting a bit strained. So we're onto the seafood ones now, are we? Don't be *shellfish*, Garaman – tell us what it's for.' He grinned at his own joke, but no one else did. 'Suit yourselves,' he grumped. 'Why's this place so important?'

Garaman dropped his shoulders mockingly.

'Oh, very well,' he said. 'If I *must*…'

'Oh you must,' encouraged the Doctor. 'You really must.'

'You don't want to have a guess? Oh come on, Doctor, you must have some idea. After all, you're a clever man.'

The Doctor was surprised.

'You mean this whole station *isn't* just a place for you lot to hide? Not a nice little pied-à-terre for you to hole up in whilst the galaxy goes to hell in a hand-basket?'

'You really think I have the patience to wait for that?'

'Well,' mused the Doctor. 'Considering it's been hiding in a black hole for all these years, you must have some pretty good temporal and gravitational shielding. You could gather all your little followers together and sit inside Sentilli, waiting for the galaxy to go to war, the machines to be defeated, and then come out – and, what, barely a month would have gone past.'

'It's always an option,' Garaman conceded. 'But no. I'm not that patient, Doctor. Nor am I that convinced that, if such a war between organics and inorganics came, that our side would be victorious.'

The Doctor thought for a moment and then pulled his face into a shrug.

'Nope, you've stumped me there. Come on – spill the

beans. What's this place for?'

'I'm disappointed, Doctor, I really am.'

'Oh, stop gloating,' the Doctor snapped. 'It's very unattractive. We all have our off days.'

Garaman thought for a moment and then nodded, beckoning to the supermodel robot. It stepped forward, silently.

'Access Garaman AC001,' he said to the robot.

Instantly, the machine raised its right arm, palm up, and pushed up the sleeve on its immaculately tailored jacket. A long, thin panel opened in its arm. And with the faint hiss of compressed air, a slender, black-and-yellow-striped cylinder rose out of the slot. Garaman took it and the panel closed before the robot lowered its arm.

'This,' Garaman said, handing the cylinder to Mesanth who took it in trembling fingers, 'is the activator.'

The Doctor deftly reached into the inside pocket of his jacket and pulled out his glasses. He popped them on his nose, pushed them right up with the tip of his finger, and peered at the device.

'The activator?'

Garaman smiled like a cat that had just trapped the biggest, juiciest mouse in the house. And then discovered it was filled with cream.

He turned to Mesanth and handed him the cylinder.

'How long will it take?' Garaman asked.

'Half an hour or so,' Mesanth answered, his voice musical with excitement. It seemed like he'd already forgotten all the deaths. The Doctor felt suddenly and strangely sad.

'Plenty of time to fill you in on the details, then,'

beamed Garaman to the Doctor. He looked up at Mesanth, clutching the activator in his trembling fingers. 'Go on – I'll be up later.'

With a last glance at the Doctor, Mesanth set off towards a broad, spiral staircase at the far side of the platform. The Doctor scanned upwards to where it reached an overhead gantry, but the darkness shrouded everything up there.

'Where's Mesanth off to, then? Anywhere nice?'

'He's off to finish installing and calibrating the activator.' Garaman almost clapped his hands together in glee. 'Ah, yes! I was just about to tell you what the activator does, wasn't I?'

'Finally,' said the Doctor, eyes rolling. 'Your master plan.'

'Yes,' said a familiar voice from the darkness. 'Tell us about your master plan, Garaman. We're all ears.'

And out of the shadows that surrounded the platform stepped Donna: behind her were Boonie, Kellique, Mother – and the little robot from Junk, the one that had threatened him.

'Donna!'

'Doctor!' laughed Donna.

'Good to see you,' the Doctor said, grinning broadly, 'although your timing could have been better. As the Ginger Goddess, I'd have thought you'd have known better.'

'Never mention that again,' she said with a raised eyebrow. 'And anyway, my timing's *always* perfect,' she insisted, as Boonie pulled a gun from the holster at his waist and aimed it fair and square at Garaman.

'But Garaman was just about to tell me his plan for

universal domination, weren't you?' He turned to Garaman who glowered at him coldly, clearly not sure what to do now.

'Mechanical!' Garaman commanded suddenly. 'Protect me!'

Moving so quickly it was almost a blur, the supermodel robot positioned itself between Boonie and Garaman, raised its arms, and began to advance on Boonie. But it had gone scarcely a step, knocking the gun from Boonie's hand and sending it flying into the darkness around them, when Mother made *her* move. Almost as swiftly as the supermodel had acted, Mother took a couple of huge steps forward and slapped the robot across the side of the head. With an almighty crash of metal, the robot's blonde head left its shoulders in a shower of sparks and went tumbling away into the darkness; the rest of its body, taking up some of the momentum of the mighty swing, flew across the platform and toppled onto one side, arms flapping about pathetically.

The little boxy robot raised its hands to its face and covered its eyes.

'Oh dear,' it muttered. 'I hate real violence. It's not like on TV at all, is it? At least there's no oil – that'd just be *gross!*'

Garaman took a step back, realising that he was outnumbered and overpowered. He glanced up into the darkness, clearly trying to see where Mesanth was.

'You know,' said the Doctor, 'I almost feel sorry for you both. I mean, all these years of planning, all this effort. And for what? The irony of being beaten by a mechanical?

Just Mesanth to sort out and we can all be home in time for tea. Now, Ms Noble, what about that hug?'

'Don't I get one too?' came another voice – and from out of the darkness stepped Li'ian, her face and the blue dress she wore smeared with dirt and oil. There was a tear in one sleeve: she looked like she'd been through the wars.

'Li'ian!' cried Donna. 'We thought you were dead!'

'How did you get off the ship?' asked Boonie incredulously.

'Oh, I imagine she used the transmat,' said the Doctor blithely. 'Once she knew that *The Sword of Justice* was about to get its edge blunted. Why don't you tell them, Li'ian?' He folded his arms and narrowed his eyes. 'Tell them how you're actually one of the Cult of Shining Darkness.'

'What?' frowned Donna, looking between the two of them.

'Oh, there's a lot of secrets round here, aren't there?' He flicked a glance at Boonie, but Li'ian gave a wry smile – before whipping a gun out of her pocket, grabbing Donna by the arm and pulling her close. She pressed the tip of the gun barrel to Donna's temple and dragged her back to the edge of the platform, making sure she could see everyone clearly, and that no one could sneak up on her.

'Ha!' exclaimed Garaman, clapping his hands together triumphantly. 'Well done, Li'ian!'

Li'ian threw him a scornful look.

'Oh shut up,' she said – and shot him, right between the eyes.

FOURTEEN

Just when she thought she had the whole thing sussed, it went and got all complicated again.

The journey from *The Sword of Justice* to the space station had been a rackety, terrifying one, even with Kellique at the thruster controls. They had no idea whether Mother had damaged the pod as she'd freed it, though. Every second of the trip, Donna had been expecting the pod to suddenly spin out of control, or begin leaking air or explode or something. And they had no idea whether Mother had managed to cling on, or whether, even now, her atomised remains were mingling with the wreckage of *The Sword*.

A tiny videoscreen had showed them their approach to the station as, with deft hands, Kellique had spun the pod about and backed it up to the station's own airlock. Fortunately, thought Donna, whoever had designed all these ships and escape pods had thought to fit them with adaptable 'universal' docks, something she wished were the case with her mobile, her camera, her mp3 player and her computer at home. When she got back, she'd be writing a few choice emails to the manufacturers…

But she needn't have worried: by the time the pod had locked on and the airlock opened, Mother was already aboard the station, waiting to greet them like an oversized, metallic bouncer. She'd almost expected the robot to raise a hand and say, 'If your name's not down, you're not coming in.'

It hadn't taken them long to find the control centre – Weiou had interfaced with the station's main computer to get directions – and here they were, waist-deep in intrigue and mystery.

Again.

Admittedly, thought Donna, she could perhaps have waited a few seconds for that little creep Garaman to explain his master plan; but strike while the iron's hot, she thought. If the gun against her head went off, it wouldn't just be the iron that was hot. *Way to go, Noble*, she thought. *Way to go.*

Only it was *Li'ian* holding the gun to her head, and Garaman lying dead at their feet. Could this galaxy get any more upside down?

'You harm a hair on her head,' said the Doctor, pocketing his specs and glaring at Li'ian, 'and even the Andromeda galaxy won't be big enough to hide in, believe me.'

'What's going on?' wailed Weiou. 'Oh dear, this isn't good, is it?'

'Not for you it isn't,' said Li'ian. 'No.'

'Donna's on our side,' Boonie protested, clearly not believing that Li'ian could be one of the Cultists.

'She's on *your* side,' Li'ian corrected him. 'Now shut up or I'll drill a hole in her head like I did with Garaman.'

Stunned, Boonie could only comply. Donna noticed Mother shifting her weight from foot to foot. She wasn't the only one that noticed.

'If Mother makes a move,' Li'ian warned, 'Donna dies. Keep that in mind.'

'What the Hell is going on, Li'ian?' Boonie demanded. 'We're on your side.'

'Oh, I don't think you were ever on the same side, were you Li'ian?' asked the Doctor, folding his arms.

'So whose side's she on?' asked Kellique, her eyes on Garaman's body.

'I think Li'ian has her own agenda, don't you? You were working with Garaman before, weren't you? Planted with the anti-Cultists to keep an eye on them, find out what they knew – and make sure they didn't get *too* close and at the same time thought they were right on it.'

Li'ian just smiled.

'You were the one that took control of our little friend over there.' He nodded in the direction of Weiou who pulled another astonished face. 'Quite a robotics expert yourself. When you showed me those records, the ones of Khnu's history, you did a good job of removing your name from them all. I might not have suspected anything.'

'So what gave her away?' asked Boonie, still clearly confused.

'You might have edited out all the textual references to yourself, but you missed one of the pictures. There's a very nice one of you and Khnu smiling together at a cybernetics conference on Cita. Lovely picture, too. And for someone so opposed to them, you were a little bit too admiring when you spoke of her achievements, as well as having rather too much knowledge about the segments of the can-opener.' He caught sight of Donna's puzzled face. 'The thing that opened up the black hole and let this little beauty out.'

'Very good, Doctor,' said Li'ian. 'Very clever. Still... too little, too late, really.'

'So why kill Garaman?' Kellique asked.

'Because he was an idiot,' Li'ian said simply. 'And because he didn't fully appreciate the potential of what we have here. Not like Khnu did.'

'Oh yes,' said the Doctor. 'That. What exactly *do* we have here? Garaman was about to explain it all when you put the final full stop to his sentence, as it were.'

Li'ian manoeuvred Donna around to make sure no one could sneak up on her.

'How much do you know about the mechanet?' Li'ian asked.

'Ooh!' said Weiou, sticking one hand in the air. 'I know! I know!'

'Go on,' said the Doctor, trying not to laugh at the little robot's enthusiasm. 'Tell us about it. What's your name?'

'I'm Weiou,' said the robot, 'and the mechanet is—'

'It's like the internet, but for robots,' cut in Donna grimly, feeling Li'ian's grip on her arm and the gun still against her head.

'Oi!' called Weiou. 'I was going to say that!' A pouty face appeared on his screen for a moment. 'It's like the internet, but for robots. Well,' Weiou added. 'For *some* robots. Us sensible ones keep away from it, apart from when we need to sync our internal clocks or download software upgrades.' He pulled another face. 'Generally, it's just full of nerds and losers complaining about how machinekind's not as good as it used to be, or circulating rumours about "organic agendas" and nonsense like that.'

'And what's your interest in it, then?' the Doctor addressed Li'ian.

'Our little appliance there's selling the mechanet short,' she said, 'although it does have a point. Its main feature is that almost every mechanical in the galaxy – apart from the most basic servitors and appliances – hook up to it at least once a week. They claim that they're all above it, like Weiou does, but they can't help firing up their transspatial links and having a quick poke about.'

Weiou's cartoon mouth had dropped open, as if in shock.

'And don't make out that you don't, Weiou,' Li'ian said. 'Robotic communications is my field, after all. When I was pretending to run diagnostics on you before, I had a good old root around in your memories. If people knew some of the things you'd been, ahem, "researching" on the mechanet they'd be *very* surprised.'

To Donna's surprise, two little patches of red swelled up on Weiou's onscreen cheeks.

'Oh stop embarrassing him,' said the Doctor defensively. 'So, this mechanet…' He paused as the realisation of Li'ian's plan hit him. 'Ahhhh… I'm ahead of you now.'

'Only just,' said Li'ian dryly. She was manoeuvring

Donna around the platform, towards the staircase up which Mesanth had disappeared.

'This activator thingy,' the Doctor continued, hands in pockets, 'it's going to give you the power to reach into the heads of almost every robot in the galaxy and turn it off, isn't it?' He pulled a face. 'The Bishop convertors – *that's* why you need them. To broadcast across the entire galaxy simultaneously takes more than a five-volt battery. Genocide at the flick of a switch.'

'That would be just too easy,' Li'ian said, cruel laughter in her voice. 'That was *his* plan.' She gestured, quickly, with the tip of her gun at Garaman's body. 'They had the right ideals, they just couldn't take them the extra step that they should have done.'

The Doctor fixed Li'ian with a steely gaze.

'That extra step… Aaaah… you don't want to just turn off all the mechanicals, do you?' He paused, narrowing his eyes. 'You want to *control* them.' He sounded almost admiring.

'Finally!' laughed Li'ian. 'Yes – why waste such a resource. Robots, mechanicals, machine intelligences – everywhere, throughout the galaxy. If I just turn them off, someone will come along and develop new ones, ones resistant to the activator. Or they'll find a way to reprogram themselves or cut off the mechanet's signals. No, I can't let that happen. Once I have control, Doctor, I have to *keep* control. I have to make sure that the machines can never again have the upper hand. And there are robot races out there that have no contact with the mechanet at all – I'll need troops to overcome *them*.'

'You take control of the galaxy, using non-organics as your army, your police force, just to make sure that your own little warped view of what's right and what's wrong prevails?'

He scratched the back of his neck thoughtfully.

'As audacious schemes go, I have to give it to you – this one's up there with the best of them.'

'From you, Doctor, that's quite a compliment.'

'It isn't meant as one.' His voice hardened. 'Have you any idea of the suffering and death you'll cause when you turn on the activator, never mind the suffering and death you'll inflict when you actually start to build your little empire of steel? All over the galaxy, maintenance robots, healthcare machines, aircraft, spacecraft – *cars* – the moment you take control of them, they'll all stop working, like that.' He snapped his fingers. 'People will die in their millions, Li'ian. And that'll only be a taste of what's to come once you start.'

All Li'ian could do was shrug. Donna clenched her jaw and started to move, but Li'ian pressed the tip of her gun back against her temple. Slowly and carefully, Li'ian was backing up the staircase, taking her with her.

'Don't try anything,' she whispered. And then, more loudly so that everyone could hear: 'You're probably weighing up whether it's worth risking Donna's life for the sake of however many it is you think will die. I'd dispute your figures, of course, but I rather suspect that my position's getting weaker by the second. Mesanth should be well advanced with the installation by now, and – of course – I'd rather like to be the one that pushes the button.'

'He's a decent sort, Mesanth,' said the Doctor. 'A bit doolally when it comes to all this organic-versus-inorganic nonsense, but I reckon that when he finds out what your plan is, how much death you'll be causing – to organics as well as non-organics – he might have a change of heart.'

'No need for him to hear any of this. By the time I decide to tell him – if I do – it'll be all done and dusted.'

Li'ian pulled Donna up a few more steps, twisting the pair of them around so that they were still facing the Doctor and the others, staring up at them from the platform.

'You do realise,' called the Doctor, 'that I can't let you do this. Donna or no Donna, I can't let you use that activator.'

'Yes, I do,' replied Li'ian as they moved up another step. 'And I know that the moment my attention's diverted, you'll be up these stairs after me. So I think that right now might be a good time for a little diversion – and a taste of what's to come.'

Donna felt Li'ian shift behind her.

'Lights!' she shouted into the darkness, and suddenly, the entire area was flooded with painfully bright light. Donna raised an arm to shelter her eyes. As she blinked, she could see her friends, down on the platform, doing the same, looking around them, wondering what was happening.

But Donna had the best view: standing in silent concentric rows around the platform were robots. Dozens and dozens and *dozens* of the blonde supermodel robots. They stretched away to the far walls of the chamber, all dressed identically, each with its geometrically perfect blonde bob and its cold, emotionless eyes.

'Mine,' Li'ian said softly so that only Donna could hear her. 'All mine. Say goodbye to your friends, Donna.'

They'd reached the gantry at the top of the staircase and Li'ian pressed the gun into the back of Donna's neck as she turned her towards an open door.

'Mechanicals!' Donna heard Li'ian shout down into the chamber. 'Deactivate audio and wireless links. Locate the five newcomers on the platform. And kill them.'

The last thing Donna saw before the door slid shut was the Doctor, looking up at her, as the robots began their advance.

FIFTEEN

'Oh my,' said Weiou, scuttling between Mother's legs, as if that might provide protection from the hundreds and hundreds of robots surrounding them.

'Oh my, indeed,' echoed the Doctor. 'And Donna still has the sonic screwdriver…'

With a sinisterly synchronised stamping of their feet, the robots drew closer, the first ones already on the steps leading up to the platform. Their cold, blue eyes stared ahead of them, utterly free of any malice or compassion. They were simply doing as they'd been ordered. It reminded him of the Jaftee on Karris – only this time it was *him* that was at the heart of it all, and he had no Ginger Goddess to protect him.

'Back!' called the Doctor, gesturing towards the spiral staircase up which Li'ian had just taken Donna. 'It's the only way out. Move!'

The Doctor noticed how Mother was turning her head this way and that, clearly trying to work out whether she could protect the rest of them at the same time as fighting off as many of the robots as she could. But the Doctor knew it was an impossible task. And he knew that *Mother* knew it was an impossible task. They were approaching from all directions, and they had the sheer weight of numbers on their side, despite Mother's bulk.

'Weiou!' the Doctor said turning to the little robot that was already clambering up the stairs. 'You're good at interfacing with stuff, aren't you? Technology, machines.' He raised an eyebrow. 'Robots?'

'Um,' replied Weiou cautiously, rotating the upper half of his body so that it faced him. 'Maybe.'

The sound of crashing came from behind him, and the Doctor turned briefly to see one of the robots flying through the air, a mass of tangled arms and legs. As he watched, Mother reached out and whacked another one, sending it careering into its fellows.

'What can you tell us about these?'

Weiou's cartoon face scrunched up in exaggerated effort.

'I can access their ID tags, but that dreadful woman's turned off all inputs, like she said.'

'And…?'

More robots crashed behind him.

'They're Meeta-Corrin humaniform servitors, model DF181B. Lipanov rating 23. That's about it. And then loads of dull stuff about the software they're running.'

At Weiou's words, there was a deep, electronic hum from Mother.

'What?' asked the Doctor, turning and looking up at

the behemoth. She'd stopped battering the robots and they were again drawing closer. Boonie and Kellique were standing on the staircase a few steps up, looking confused.

'Meeta-Corrin,' said Boonie. 'That's the company that made Mother. It's where we rescued her from.'

The Doctor turned back to Mother as her head turned slowly, as if she were seeing the robots in a new light.

Suddenly, in front of her – and just visible to the Doctor from where he stood – a rectangle of pink light flickered, like an old-fashioned TV set warming up. Mother had activated her projector.

>THEY ARE RUNNING SOFTWARE CONTAINING HEURISTICS DERIVED FROM ME.

It took the Doctor a second to realise what Mother was saying.

'These are your *children*?'

>GRANDCHILDREN MIGHT BE MORE ACCURATE.

The Doctor raised his eyebrows, suddenly realising that this revelation could place them in a very dangerous position: Mother was the only thing that stood between the robots and them, and now she'd discovered that they were her grandchildren.

'You must be very proud,' he said dryly, as Mother actually took a step back, away from the approaching horde of blonde hair and sharp tailoring. 'Any chance you could, oh, I dunno, tell them to go to their rooms? Sometimes works, you know.'

>LI'IAN ANTICIPATED SUCH A POSSIBILITY, flickered the red letters. Beyond them, the robots drew closer.

HAD SHE NOT DISABLED PRIMARY AND AUDITORY INPUTS, I COULD HAVE ACCESSED ROOT COMMAND STRUCTURES.

The robots were now moving across the platform, their steps still eerily in sync, their eyes cold and dead. Mother took a step forward and swiped another three of the robots off the platform and into their comrades. The others stepped over the fallen ones and kept on coming.

'Mother' said the Doctor quietly, putting his hand on her steel arm. 'You don't have to do this, you know. Not now we know…'

>I KNOW.

The letters winked silently for a second.

>IF I DO NOT DEFEND US, WE WILL BE KILLED.

'They're your grandchildren,' the Doctor reminded her, waving Boonie, Kellique and Weiou further up the staircase.

>THEY ARE ALSO NON-SENTIENT MECHANICALS. THEY ARE INCAPABLE OF FEELING PAIN OR DISTRESS OR BETRAYAL.

'I know,' said the Doctor gently. 'But you're not.'

Another robot got within reach of Mother, and with a disturbing casualness, she reached out and swatted it away: it went flying into the ones behind it, scattering them like bowling pins. Silently, they clambered back to their feet and resumed their advance. It seemed like Mother had made her decision.

>GO, Mother flashed. STOP LI'IAN.

'I'm not leaving you. There must be—'

He stopped dead as something occurred to him –

something, in hindsight, that seemed blindingly obvious. Ironically so.

'Mother!' he said urgently, his words tumbling over each other. 'Access to their command pathways – how do you get it? I mean, what would you have to do – alpha-numerics?'

>A 256-CHARACTER STRING TRANSMITTED TO THEM.

'Ha!' cried the Doctor triumphantly.

'What's with the "Ha!"?' scowled Boonie from the top of the staircase. 'They're not accepting wireless commands and they're as deaf as posts—' Boonie stopped as he realised what had occurred to the Doctor. A grin broke across his face. 'But they're not *blind*!'

'Correctamundo – oh…' The Doctor's face fell. 'I was never going to say that again. But yes, they're not blind. That's one input that Li'ian couldn't disable – not if she didn't want them walking into walls. Mother! Is there any chance that you could have a word with the grandkids – *show* them the access code?'

'Doctor!' Boonie called down the staircase. 'You realise that it won't just send the servitors to sleep, don't you?'

'What?'

'If Mother sends the code, they'll shut down – for good.'

'Oh.' The Doctor ran his hand through his hair and looked up at Mother. 'Your call,' he whispered. 'We'll understand if you don't want to, you know.'

>YOU THINK OF THIS AS MURDER?

The Doctor didn't know how to answer.

>THINK OF THEM AS OUT-OF-CONTROL LAWNMOWERS.

'Well,' said the Doctor, not at all convinced. 'When you put it like that…'

Mother gave a satisfied little hum – as she felled another couple of the blonde robots – and suddenly a great long string of numbers and letters flickered across her holographic screen, faster than the eye could follow.

'Don't worry,' the Doctor called up to the others. 'They're fast readers.'

The code continued to scroll along the screen, the characters just a blur now, as Mother turned on the spot, at the very foot of the staircase, to make sure all the supermodel robots had seen it.

In waves, the robots just stopped.

No fuss, no noise, they just *stopped*.

First the ones at the front, the ones who had the best view of Mother's projection. And as she turned, more and more of them saw the command string. Silently, and instantly, Mother's code infiltrated the robots' processor cores, and turned them off for good.

The silence was deafening.

'I'm sorry you had to do that,' the Doctor said, looking up at Mother. 'But thank you. Who better than a grandmother to know what buttons to press to shut the grandchildren up, eh?'

'Oh,' said Weiou, peering out from behind Kellique. 'Yes!'

He punched the air.

***

'You know what *really* gets me,' said Donna as Li'ian pushed her through the door into a room, 'is that I fell for it.'

'Don't beat yourself up,' Li'ian said with a cold smile, motioning with the gun for Donna to move away. They were in a brightly lit room, more like an operating theatre than the grungy industrial theme that the rest of the station seemed to have been decorated in. It lay off a long corridor at the top of the staircase. From down below, Donna could still hear the sound of the robots, stomping and crashing. So far she'd heard no screams or sounds that anyone had been hurt – anyone organic. But with the sheer numbers of supermodels, that could only be a matter of time.

'And what's worse,' she added, fixing the surprised Mesanth with a hard glare, 'is that the Doctor did too.'

'Which only proves my point,' Li'ian said. 'If it's that easy to make you think that *I* believe that mechanicals are sentient, why is it so hard for *you* to believe that *they*'ve pulled the same trick with organics. I fooled you; they are fooling everyone. Well,' she added with a smug smile. 'Not everyone. Mesanth – how're you doing?'

The lizard was standing at a complex-looking console, all three of his hands moving over the controls. Donna could see the striped cylinder of the activator, looking like a cross between a wasp and a particularly large sausage, on the console in front of him.

'I'm not happy,' he said, his normally animated voice flat and controlled.

'You don't have to be happy,' Li'ian said, waving the gun casually, making a point. 'You just have to do the job.'

'No, Mesanth, you don't,' cut in Donna. 'You don't have

to do what this mad cow says at all. *Come on!* Think about it – think of all the death—'

There was a sharp, high-pitched buzz and a section of the wall alongside Donna exploded in tiny sparks, leaving an acrid smell in the air and a wisp of smoke.

'Shut up,' said Li'ian, waving the gun that had just almost killed her. 'Mesanth might have scruples about killing you, but I don't.'

Donna glared at her, and then looked back at Mesanth, imploring him with her eyes not to continue.

'Where's Garaman?' asked Mesanth, casting his eyes to the window that ran along the length of the laboratory.

'He got cold feet,' Li'ian said, holding Donna's gaze as she spoke, unspoken threat in her eyes.

'About what?'

'It doesn't matter now – he's no longer part of the plan. And the plan's… changed.'

'How?' Mesanth's voice was getting higher in pitch. Donna could tell he was on the edge of being hysterical again. His hands trembled as he operated the controls in front of him.

'We're not just going to turn off the mechanicals,' she said, keeping her eyes steady on his. 'We're going to take control of them.'

'What? Why? What was wrong with Khnu's original plan?' Mesanth's voice shot up half an octave.

'Oh, you idiot, Mesanth,' sighed Li'ian. 'That *was* Khnu's original plan.'

'What?' Mesanth's voice jumped up another half an octave.

'Well, *our* plan. She thought it through: turn off all the mechanicals and before you know it, someone would come up with a workaround. Days, weeks – and we'd have a whole new load of mechanicals immune to the activator. We'd be back where we started. Khnu knew that this was the one chance to gain control – and *keep* control.'

'But we could do something,' he said plaintively. 'Work something out…' He tailed off, not knowing how to finish the sentence.

'You're starting to think like the promechanicals,' said Li'ian tiredly. 'Before you know it you'll be starting to doubt your own convictions. This is how they work, Mesanth.' She tapped the gun against her own temple. 'They get in *here*, start making you doubt what you believe.' She waved the gun at the console and the activator. 'Just finish, Mesanth, and then we can leave here – go out into the galaxy, heads held high. Liberators.'

Donna opened her mouth to say something, hoping that the embers of decency that she'd seen in Mesanth could be fanned into a flame; but Li'ian saw her and aimed the gun fair and square at her head.

'One more word,' she said softly.

The Doctor shooed Kellique, Boonie and Weiou up the stairs ahead of them.

'I'm sorry,' he said to Mother, surveying the chamber full of fallen and frozen robots. 'If there had been another way…'

>NO APOLOGIES NECESSARY, flashed Mother. THEY WERE NOT SENTIENT AND THERE IS MORE AT STAKE

THAN MY FEELINGS.

The Doctor shook his head and rubbed the back of his neck.

'You know,' he said, 'I'm not sure I'll ever really understand the machine mind.'

>I KNOW, replied Mother. WE ARE MUCH MORE COMPLEX THAN YOU ORGANICS.

The Doctor narrowed his eyes.

'You have a very dry sense of humour, you know that?' He reached up high and slapped her on the back. 'Come on – let's go and sort Li'ian out before she plunges your galaxy into a somewhat less-than-shining darkness!'

The others were waiting for them when they arrived: Mother had found it easier to clamber up the *outside* of the spiral staircase because of her bulk. The corridor, though, was high enough for her to stand upright.

It didn't take them long to find Li'ian, Donna and Mesanth: they were in a brightly lit room, a laboratory, with a huge window facing out onto the corridor. Li'ian gave a start when she saw them, and the Doctor could see the fury flare in her eyes.

'Mother didn't take kindly to her grandchildren running amok,' the Doctor called through the intercom set into the doorframe. 'Had to have a quiet word with them. They're taking a nap.'

'Doctor!' called Donna, waving.

'Destiny seems to want to keep us apart,' said the Doctor. 'Like Romeo and Juliet.'

Donna flashed a none-too-convincing smile.

'Don't push it,' she said.

'Fair enough. Anyway, Li'ian, I take it you're holding Donna at gunpoint and will threaten to shoot her if we don't go away and leave you in peace. That about sum it up?'

'It'll do,' agreed Li'ian, showing the Doctor her gun.

A few metres away, Mesanth busied himself with the activator, risking a nervous glance over his shoulder. He was visibly shaking.

'You don't have to do this—' the Doctor started to say.

'Been there,' Donna cut in. 'Done that. Got the brush-off.'

'And in case you're thinking of getting Mother to smash her way in,' called Li'ian, 'I should point out the reinforcement that's gone into this room's construction. Nothing short of a bomb will get you in here. And in, ooh, about ten minutes, the activator will be ready and it'll be too late.' She smiled, almost sadly.

The Doctor shoved his hands deep in his pockets and shrugged.

'Well it's a good job that we've *got* a bomb, then, isn't it?'

'We've got a bomb?' said Weiou, who kept jumping up and down in order to see what was going on in the activator room. 'Where?'

The Doctor looked at Boonie.

'Are you going to tell them, or shall I?'

'What?' Boonie suddenly looked very evasive. 'What bomb?'

'A *bomb*?' echoed Kellique.

'And not just *any* bomb,' said the Doctor. 'An *antimatter* bomb. An antimatter bomb that will take out this whole station.' He paused, his eyes wide. 'That's a *big* bomb.'

'You're bluffing,' laughed Li'ian. 'And not very well.'

'A *bomb?*' repeated Kellique pointedly.

'Tell her, Boonie,' said the Doctor.

Boonie just looked from the Doctor to Kellique – and then to Mother, where his gaze stayed.

'I don't know what you're talking about,' he said.

'Oh, I think you do,' countered the Doctor. 'I think you know exactly what I mean. Go on, Boonie – tell us all about the bomb. The one that you hid inside Mother.'

There was a stunned silence: everyone's eyes flicked to Mother and then back to Boonie.

'What? I don't know what he's talking about. He's mad.'

But there was a tremor, an uncertainty in his voice that kept everyone's eyes on him.

'You might as well tell them, Boonie,' said the Doctor. 'In a few minutes, Li'ian's going to turn that thing on and millions and billions of the machines that you've devoted the last few years of your life to protecting are going to die. It might be the only way to stop her, mightn't it? That's why you put it there, after all. No need to be a retiring bride on the day of your wedding.' He glanced through the window at Donna and pulled a face. 'Not my best metaphor, but still…'

Boonie looked at them all, and his shoulders sagged. 'I was going to tell you,' he said awkwardly, looking up at Mother.

'What?' twittered Weiou, turning this way and that to

try to follow the conversation. 'Tell who what?'

'Were you?' asked the Doctor of Boonie. 'When were you going to find the right time to tell Mother that you'd hidden a bomb inside her? Not the kind of thing you can just throw into the conversation, is it? "Oooh, look at that beautiful nebula – oh, and by the way, there are a few grams of antimatter tucked away inside you waiting for me to detonate them." Bit of a showstopper, that one, isn't it?'

'How did you know?' asked Boonie, his eyes narrow and suspicious.

'When I was aboard your ship, me and Mother had a bit of a chat – and I happened to notice it.'

Boonie looked shocked – understandably, thought the Doctor.

'I'm sorry,' he said, falteringly, to Mother. 'I didn't think I'd ever have to… use it.'

>THAT IS HARD TO BELIEVE, Mother flashed in crimson letters. YOU MUST HAVE CONSIDERED THE POSSIBILITY THAT YOU *WOULD* HAVE TO USE IT.

'It's not like that,' Boonie said, clasping his head in frustration. 'It was just an insurance policy. I didn't know what the Cultists were up to – I had no idea what was going to happen. I had to…' He shook his head, realising how weak his own arguments sounded. 'I had to be able to stop them.'

>WE WERE FRIENDS.

'We were – we *are*.' Boonie shook his head, unable to make eye contact with Mother.

>FRIENDS DO NOT TURN EACH OTHER INTO BOMBS.

'If I could have implanted it in myself, I would have done.'

>THAT MAY BE TRUE. BUT YOU COULD HAVE TOLD ME.

'I was scared you'd say no,' Boonie said. He blinked away the beginnings of tears and rubbed his nose with the back of his hand.

>THAT IS A RISK WITH TELLING THE TRUTH. BUT IT IS ALWAYS PREFERABLE TO A LIE. THAT YOU WOULD BE WILLING TO KILL ME, EVEN IN THE PURSUIT OF PREVENTING THE CULT FROM ACHIEVING THEIR ENDS, IS A DISTURBING THOUGHT. PERHAPS YOU ARE CLOSER TO THE CULT OF SHINING DARKNESS THAN YOU BELIEVE.

'No, no. I'm nothing like them.'

>WOULD YOU HAVE BEEN SO WILLING TO IMPLANT THE BOMB IN AN ORGANIC? MY MACHINE NATURE MAKES ME DIFFERENT. DISPOSABLE?

'It's not like that,' Boonie pleaded again. 'If I'd ever had to use it, I would have been there by your side, right at the end. I couldn't have put it in myself – it would have shown up on all sorts of scanners. Inside you, no one would have been able to tell that it wasn't part of you.'

'What's going on?' called Li'ian, and the Doctor realised that from where she stood she wouldn't be able to see Mother's display screen: all she would have heard would have been Boonie's side of the conversation, relayed through the intercom.

'Oh, just talking amongst ourselves,' the Doctor said airily. 'Antimatter bombs, friendship, that sort of thing.

Getting a bit soapy to be quite honest, but hey, what can you do? With you in a mo.'

'Explosions always make me feel bilious,' muttered Weiou. 'There's not going to be one, is there?'

>THAT IS BOONIE'S DECISION, Mother said. HE HAS THE ACTIVATION CODE FOR THE BOMB. IF HE CHOOSES TO USE IT, I CANNOT STOP HIM.

Boonie looked from Mother to the Doctor.

'What do we do?' he asked, almost in a whisper. His face was blank, streaked with tears that cut pale tracks through the dirt and grime of their escape from *The Sword of Justice*.

'Dunno,' said the Doctor casually, rubbing the back of his neck. 'You're the one with the code for the bomb.' He rapped on the window. 'Mesanth – sorry to bother you, but how long have we got left before your little Armageddon-o-matic kicks in?'

'Five minutes,' said Mesanth. He didn't look happy. Li'ian threw him an angry look.

'Doctor!' called Donna. 'I'm sure you've got everything well in hand out there; but all this talk of bombs and stuff is making me just a *bit* edgy.'

'He's bluffing,' said Li'ian. 'I know his type.'

'And you're very good at that, aren't you,' the Doctor said sarcastically, 'knowing *types*. That's how you think, isn't it? Forget individuals, forget people – everyone's just a *type* to you.'

The Doctor noticed the look of concern that passed across Li'ian's face. Keeping the gun aimed at Donna, she moved over to join Mesanth at his workstation and whispered something to him.

'Whisperers tell lies,' the Doctor taunted.

Li'ian ignored him.

'By my watch,' the Doctor said, looking at his wrist, 'I'd say we've got about four and a half minutes before Mad Mary in there flicks the switch. How long is the timer on the bomb?'

Boonie lifted his eyes from the floor. 'A minute.'

'Okaaaay,' said the Doctor. 'So we've got three and a half minutes to bicker and argue and point blaming fingers before we have to decide.' He took a deep breath. 'Good – plenty of time then – off you go: bicker away!'

He folded his arms and leaned against the wall. Everyone stared at him in silence.

'Go,' Boonie said suddenly. 'All of you, go, find a shuttle – me and Mother will stay.'

The Doctor's shoulders fell.

'Not the heroic sacrifice bit?' he said wearily. 'Isn't that a bit old hat?'

'Just go,' Boonie repeated. 'We'll finish this place off, won't we, Mother?'

He looked up at her, and the Doctor could see that there were tears in his eyes again.

>YES, she said, after a moment's consideration. I AM NOT HAPPY ABOUT THE DECEPTION, BUT YES, WE WILL. THIS IS MORE IMPORTANT THAN EITHER OF US.

'All of you,' Boonie said urgently. '*Go.*'

The Doctor took a deep breath.

'Well it's very nice of you to offer to blow yourselves up, but we're all in this together, aren't we?'

'Are we?' squeaked Weiou worriedly.

'We are,' said the Doctor firmly. He looked through the window at Donna.

'You ready to be blown to smithereens to preserve galactic peace, Donna?'

'Oh yeah,' she called back blithely. 'Always. Just like Pompeii all over again, isn't it?'

'Go on, then,' said Li'ian, smiling again. 'I dare you.'

'D'you hear that, Boonie? Mother? Li'ian's daring you! Not going to let her get away with that, are you?'

Boonie looked up at Mother and then around at the little group gathered in the corridor. He caught the Doctor's eyes.

'Activation code,' Boonie said, his voice audibly trembling. 'Shining Darkness 111.'

Mother's virtual screen flickered: >CODE ACCEPTED. CONFIRM?

For a moment, Boonie paused, and the Doctor wondered if he was actually going to go through with it.

'Confirm,' he said.

Abruptly, Mother's screen flickered again and turned blood red. In large digits, the number 60 appeared in white, and as they watched, flicked over to 59. Mother turned so that Li'ian could see the display

'It's a bluff,' she said, although the Doctor could see that she suddenly wasn't so sure.

'Your choice,' said the Doctor. 'Fifty five seconds to decide whether it is or it isn't. You might be right – it might all be a clever plan cooked up between us.' He examined his fingernails. 'Or it might not.'

Li'ian leaned in close to Mesanth and said something urgently, although the Doctor couldn't catch the words. Donna, he saw, was looking for a chance to grab the gun from Li'ian, but when she caught sight of him, he gave a tiny shake of his head.

'You're right,' said Li'ian suddenly, moving to another control panel. 'It might – and it might not. And the moment I surrender, I imagine you'll cancel the countdown.'

'It can't be cancelled,' Boonie said grimly.

'What?' wailed Weiou. 'But I thought that was the plan! Oh my!'

'Seriously?' asked the Doctor, his eyes wide.

'Seriously,' Boonie said.

Kellique's eyes matched the Doctor's.

'We're going to die,' she gasped, grabbing Mother's leg for support. 'What about escape shuttles?'

'Sorry,' said the Doctor. 'I don't think –' he checked his watch again '– eighteen seconds would be enough to get to one.'

There was a flurry of movement from within the room. Li'ian and Mesanth were unplugging bits and pieces from the console and gathering them up, including the waspy cylinder of the activator.

'Probably not,' Li'ian said grimly. 'But it'll be enough to transmat back to our ship. With this.' She held up the activator as she jabbed at a control panel and spoke at it.

'Bring us back!' she said, her eyes glinting triumphantly.

'Oh great!' enthused the Doctor – without much enthusiasm. 'Just when the party's getting started!' He folded his arms grumpily. 'Go on then, off you go. Leave us here to clear up the cans and empty the ashtrays.'

'I still think you're bluffing, Doctor,' Li'ian said, making sure she had all her bits and pieces. 'But if the station hasn't blown up in a few seconds, we'll be back. And if it *has*...' She gave a great big shrug. 'It might take us a few weeks or months to hook the activator into another transmitter powerful enough to do the job, but we'll get there. We've come too far to be stopped now.' A shimmering, snowy glow enveloped her and Mesanth. 'And when we've finished in our galaxy,' she called, her voice fading into sizzling static, 'maybe we'll pay a visit to yours...'

The glow built to a crescendo and then faded abruptly. Li'ian and Mesanth were gone. Everyone turned to Mother and her countdown.

>5, it said.

'Stop it!' cried Weiou. 'Stop it! Go on – I know that's your plan. I *know* it is!'

But the Doctor just looked down at the little robot and shook his head.

'Sorry, Weiou. Boonie was right. I can't.'

>4

>3

>2

Inside the room, Donna rushed to the door, jabbing at the buttons to open it.

>1

>0

SIXTEEN

'What happened?' asked Ogmunee, the moment that Mesanth and Li'ian materialised.

'View screen on,' Li'ian barked. 'Show me the station!'

Ogmunee pulled a sniffy face but turned to the display controls anyway.

'Oh,' he said, suddenly remembering something. 'This thing I took from the Doctor.' He picked up a shiny red sphere, the size of a tangerine, from the console. 'I've not been able to open it. It's just started flashing. Any idea what it—'

In the vacuum of space, exploding spaceships make no sound: there's no air to carry the vibration. But anyone watching the *Dark Light* wouldn't have needed to hear it to know what immense energies had just been liberated.

Within the red sphere, a magnetic containment field cut out, and a few billion atoms of matter were allowed, at long last, to mingle with a few billion atoms of antimatter.

It was like long-lost friends meeting at a party. A very loud, very noisy party. The sort of party that has the neighbours banging on the walls.

A flower of intense blue-white light erupted at the front of the ship, expanding like a star, expanding outwards and outwards, consuming the rest of the vessel in less than a second, blasting the remains far, far out into space until, like dying sparks, they flickered and went dark.

Not even looking at Mother's screen, not wanting to know the exact moment that her life ended, just wanting it to be quick and painless, Donna pressed herself against the Doctor in a hug that nearly knocked him off his feet. She buried her face in his chest, holding her breath, waiting for the end.

As she waited, she felt a gentle tap on her shoulder and looked up to see the Doctor looking down at her. A smile twitched at the corner of his mouth.

'Oh you *git!*' she said after a moment, pulling away and punching him in the chest. 'It *was* a bluff, wasn't it?' She stared at him, open-mouthed. 'You complete and utter *git!*'

'No,' he said, the smile subsiding. 'It wasn't. And yes, I probably am.' He grinned rakishly. 'A bit.'

Donna looked up at Mother. Her screen had vanished. She looked around. Everyone was either staring in shock or just looking puzzled. And of them all, Boonie looked the most puzzled.

'How did you…?' he said to Mother.

'She didn't,' answered the Doctor, popping on his specs

and slipping past them to enter the room where Li'ian and Mesanth had been working on the activator. They followed him in.

'So we're all dead and this is... the final upload?' whispered Weiou. He glanced at the Doctor and then, magically, a pair of glasses just like the Doctor's, appeared on his cartoon face. He reached out to touch a wall as if he thought his fingers might go through it. 'Oh my.'

'If it is,' said the Doctor, playing with the controls, 'it's a bit unimaginative, isn't it? There!' He waved at a screen on the console.

The screen showed the blackness of space, peppered with a few cold, hard stars.

'What's that, then?' asked Weiou.

'That's what's left of the Cult of Shining Darkness. Ironic, eh?'

'Uh?' Weiou leaned back to look up at him, peering over his specs.

'They've gone?' said Kellique. 'Where?'

'Where we're all going to go in the end.' The Doctor sounded almost regretful.

'They're *dead*?' asked Donna.

The Doctor just narrowed his lips.

'The bomb,' said Boonie. 'Mother's bomb. It was on *their* ship, wasn't it?'

'I did tell Ogmunee that he really, *really* didn't want it,' said the Doctor, but there was no humour in his voice. 'But some people just won't listen, will they?'

'How?' Boonie shook his head. 'I mean, when...?'

'When I found it inside her. It didn't fit. Not just

physically, but it was all wrong for her. So I…' He pulled a slightly sheepish face. 'Pocketed it. She didn't even notice it was there, never mind when it wasn't. And then Ogmunee took it off me.'

Donna's eyes went wide.

'Can I just say,' she said, 'that if you're ever checking me over and decide to remove one of my internal organs, *on a whim*, I'll have you struck off.' She fixed him with a twinkly glare. 'You remember that, *Doctor*.'

'That's one thing you can say for organic life forms – they don't cope well with having bits of them taken out.' The Doctor took a deep breath. 'Still… Live by the sword, die by the sword.'

A heavy silence descended on them all as they stared at the screen. Suddenly, the Doctor leaned forward and squinted at it, before his fingers did a little dance over the keyboard. The image leaped towards them: floating in the midst of the darkness was a familiar, welcoming shape.

'Thank god!' sighed Donna, staring at the tumbling blue box. 'I was trying to work out how to tell you that I'd lost the TARDIS.'

'She's a hard thing to lose – we can use one of the station's shuttles to pick her up. And sooner rather than later. Wouldn't want her falling into Sentilli, now, would we?'

Donna linked her arm with the Doctor's. 'No, we wouldn't. Let's go home, yeah?'

'Home,' agreed the Doctor. 'Give me a few minutes to get the engines going – we'll send this thing back into Sentilli without its shields on. It'll be gone before you know it. And after we collect the TARDIS and a quick stop-off to take our friends back to their homes, I think the old Milky Way beckons, don't you? Where's it going to be, ladies and gentlemen? Uhlala? Dallendaf? Or…'

'Pasquite!' cried Weiou suddenly. 'Let's go to Pasquite! Can we? Can we?'

'What's on Pasquite?' asked the Doctor.

Weiou rolled his eyes behind his fake glasses.

'D'uh!' he said. 'Only the bestest machine theme park in the galaxy. They've got a simulator that shows you what it's like to be organic – all that Squidgie stuff. It's really gruesome, with blood and innards and sick and—'

The Doctor raised a hand to cut the little robot off. 'Sounds rather fun! Pasquite it is,' he grinned.

SEVENTEEN

'Is that the end of them, then – the Cult of Shining Darkness?'

Donna and the Doctor stood by the TARDIS and watched the bizarre little group, led by a jumping, squeaking Weiou (who'd clearly become so attached to his new specs that Donna suspected he'd be wearing them for ever), head off into the distance. In the valley below them was the biggest theme park she'd ever seen. From a long way off, they could hear the cheers and screams from a thousand mechanicals, all keen to find out what it was like to be a Squidgie.

'Shouldn't think so,' said the Doctor. 'It's a state of mind more than an organisation. There'll be millions more like them out there. Thinking the same, mean-spirited, tiny-minded thoughts. Scared of anything that's different, that they don't understand. And they'll always be there, ready to blame someone else for the state of the universe.'

Donna sighed and linked her arm through his.

He looked at her. 'You OK?'

Donna pulled a 'maybe' face, gazing down into the valley.

'You go through life, you know,' she said. 'Thinking you're a good person. Well, maybe not always a *good* person. Sometimes just not a *bad* person. You get up every day, go to work or college or whatever,' she added. 'You watch the telly, go on holiday. All that stuff. And you just assume it's the way it is. What your mum and dad tell you, what you see on the news, what you read in the papers. You don't question it, unless it's something about Posh's latest frock, or the Royals or what-have-you. You just, y'know, take it all in, thinking that anyone who thinks different is wrong.'

'Welllll,' said the Doctor slowly. 'They usually are. Especially when you're a Ginger Goddess.'

Donna banged her head against his shoulder.

'Nah,' she said dismissively. 'It's not all that, godhood.'

She paused and breathed in the alien air of Pasquite, so full of *strangeness* that it almost hurt. 'Travelling with you...' Donna stopped. 'Travelling with you, seeing all this stuff, risking life and limb – it scares the willies out of me, you know that.'

The Doctor raised cautionary eyebrows.

'We can always go home, you know. Back to Chiswick, back to temping, holidays in Egypt – although I'd recommend Mexico, by the way – back to normality...'

Donna smiled and shook her head.

'Meeting all these robots – all these machines, all these aliens...' She paused. 'What *is* "normal" anyway?'

The Doctor pointed to little group, a few hundred yards away: two machines, looking a bit like upright sunbeds, were walking along. On their shoulders were two kids – two Squidgie kids – laughing and squealing as the sunbeds leaned this way and that, pretending they were about to drop them.

'*That's* normal,' he said. 'Just people, being people.'

They stood in silence for a while, watching Pasquite's yellow sun drift towards the horizon, listening to the noise, breathing in the smells of food and flowers and oil.

'People,' echoed Donna. 'Just people.'

Acknowledgements

Thanks, as ever, to my faithful proof-monkeys – Stuart Douglas, Simon Forward, Michael Robinson, Paul Dale Smith and Nick Wallace.

To Justin Richards for giving me another bite of the cherry.

To everyone who enjoyed my other *Doctor Who* novels.

To Mark Morris and Simon Messingham – welcome back on board.

To Steve Tribe for his eagle eyes.

And to Russell T Davies and his team for giving us all back such a wonderful playground.

Oh my!

India in 1947 is a country in the grip of chaos – a country torn apart by internal strife. When the Doctor and Donna arrive in Calcutta, they are instantly swept up in violent events.

Barely escaping with their lives, they discover that the city is rife with tales of 'half-made men', who roam the streets at night and steal people away. These creatures, it is said, are as white as salt and have only shadows where their eyes should be.

With help from India's great spiritual leader, Mohandas 'Mahatma' Gandhi, the Doctor and Donna set out to investigate these rumours.

What is the real truth behind the 'half-made men'? Why is Gandhi's role in history under threat? And has an ancient, all-powerful god of destruction really come back to wreak his vengeance upon the Earth?

The Doctor Trap

by Simon Messingham

ISBN 978 1 846 07558 0

UK £6.99 US $11.99/$14.99 CDN

Sebastiene was perhaps once human. He might look like a nineteenth-century nobleman, but in truth he is a ruthless hunter. He likes nothing more than luring difficult opposition to a planet, then hunting them down for sport. And now he's caught them all – from Zargregs to Moogs, and even the odd Eternal…

In fact, Sebastiene is after only one more prize. For this trophy, he knows he is going to need help. He's brought together the finest hunters in the universe to play the most dangerous game for the deadliest quarry of them all.

They are hunting for the last of the Time Lords
– the Doctor.